THE DRAGON AND THE LUMBERJACK

The Thornhill Series

Book II

S W Ellenwood

Cover Design by Jerome Kremers

ISBN: 9781720011385
Independently published

www.swellenwood.com

Dedicated to the Men who helped me grow
Through the year I wrote this book:
Clay K.
Clinton J.
Daniel L.
Daniel M.
Daniel S.
(Yes, I know a Lot of Daniels)
James O.
Jon-Luke H.
Hunter T.

Chapter 1

Prison Food

Li Shang Lóng was held against the cafeteria wall by two Spaniards while the Italian approached him with a large broken piece of glass in his hand. The cafeteria was in an uproar. Twenty prisoners yelled in four different languages as the Italian prepared to cut Li open like a fish. Li struggled violently, his thin arms getting him nowhere as the large, dark-haired Spaniards held him back with shaved arms. Li didn't regret calling them cute boys. However, he did think he might have gone a little too far in calling the blond Italian a Nazi, though he thought he deserved it. None of that mattered at the moment as the Italian walked closer, looking for blood.

"You know what we do with rabid dogs like you back home?" he asked Li in Spanish.

"Sleep with them? That would explain a lot."

The Italian stopped in his tracks, while the whole prison cafeteria let out a gasp.

"Damn!" said a man in the back that made a few prisoners laugh under their breaths, while the other Italians clenched their fists. Even the Spaniards loosened up their grips and widened their eyes at the insult, which was enough for Li.

"SHUT UP!" the Italian shouted as his face burned red. He lunged at Li, swinging his hand back to drive the glass as deep as he physically could into the Asian's gut, this move left him defenseless, giving Li what he wanted. Li held on to the Spaniards and lifted himself up, throwing his foot into the air and kicking the Italian straight in the face, sending him flat on his back. The Spaniards got caught by surprise and were brought to their knees. Li wiggled out of their grips as the Italian got back on his feet. All the prisoners in the area formed a bigger circle around them. Li stood near the edge of the circle with the Italian still holding on to his weapon of glass charging him, his broken nose bleeding profusely. Li sidestepped to dodge the first swipe and jumped back to avoid the second while landing another kick on him. The Italian staggered back; behind him prisoners were parting for something. The Italian cursed Li as he wiped away the blood from his nose and prepared for another attack, which was stopped short as four prison guards tackled him. An officer walked into the circle and observed everyone, like an annoyed parent.

"Someone tell me what happened here," he commanded. Younger officers walked around the ring trying to imitate his authority. Everyone stood in silence as the officer in charge looked around. Li slowly tried to melt back into the crowd - his pride had hit its limit - but the two Spaniards pushed him back into the center of the circle, gaining the attention of the officer.

"You know something about this?" The officer pointed at the bloody-nosed Italian accusingly.

Li scanned the Italian as the guards pulled him up to his feet. "Well, it all started with this hysterical joke."

The Italian shouted in rage and tried to charge Li again. He didn't get far as the officers halted his lunge. Li flinched and chuckled at the Italian's failed attack.

"What's your name?" the officer demanded.

"Li Shang Lóng." Li held a joke inside him as he lowered his head. He had learned the hard way to pick his fights, though he still wasn't the best at it.

The officer chuckled. "Congrats, some American just bailed you out. You can go."

Li's head snapped up and he said, "Really?" The crowd had a similar reaction of disbelief.

"Did I stutter?" snapped the officer. Li shook his head. Another officer near the door motioned Li to come, which he did. The Italian and two Spaniards watched Li quickly leave the cafeteria with wide eyes and tight jaws.

Li thought later a wink would have been a great exit, but didn't think of it then as he only focused on following the officer through hallways to the room he was booked in. The clerk at the desk gave him his personal belongings: a broken wristwatch, an empty wallet, and a red ring with a carved dragon matching the tattoo on his shoulder.

"So, who paid for it?" Li asked the officer as a loud buzz sounded and the steel doors opened to Li's freedom.

"He did," the police officer responded, pointing to a handsome American with a vintage slicked-back haircut and a thick, groomed beard. The American, leaning on a red Jaguar sports car, introduced himself as Jack Montferrand. An alias. His real name was Thomas Thornhill.

Chapter 2

Six Pack

Six months had passed since Jack left the United States and his name, Thomas Thornhill, behind. Six months since the liquidation of Glass from the NSA, after the massacre and fire that was labeled 'accidental', causing the doors to that place to be closed for the last time. Six months since Mallory, Jack's fiancé, died. He still dreamed about her at least once a week. Six long months of searching for Li Shang Lóng across all of Europe, from the top of skyscrapers to the scum of sewers and all in between. Li, also known under the alias of John Wu, was the only lead Crumwell gave him before his death by Jack's hands six months ago. As Li walked out, Jack felt like he was finally making progress to finding The Twelve.

"Li Shang Lóng?" he asked as Li approached him in blue jeans and a white v-neck.

"Yeah. You the American that bailed me?" Li's eyes squinted as the late afternoon sun beat down on them. He stood a head shorter than Jack with short, black hair styled in the messy look.

"Yeah, Jack Montferrand." Jack held out his hand. Li looked at Jack's hand, and then his eyes as they lay hidden behind dark Ray-Ban sunglasses.

Li got right to the point. "What do you want?"

Jack lowered his hand and opened the passenger door for Li. "You're welcome," Jack responded. Li watched him and then the car. Jack could tell Li didn't trust him, but he could tell Li was curious.

"How can I know that you aren't some kidnapper or hit man?" asked Li as he looked back up at him.

"Because if anyone wanted you dead, you would already be dead in there." Jack nodded to the prison Li just left.

"So, you're a kidnapper? I should have known. Some American hears I'm in some puny jail cell in Spain, and you think to yourself 'that shouldn't be too hard for a smart and strong American like me.'" Li put on an American accent with a southern twang.

Jack crossed his arms and smiled. "I wouldn't know who to call if I did want to kidnap you, that's sort of why I'm here."

Li crossed his arms. "You want my contacts?" His face grew serious.

"Given my circumstance," Jack said, "it would be helpful."

"How do I know you aren't a cop?"

"Listen, I've worked with crooked cops, and no cop is paid enough to travel halfway around the world to bail someone out just to get info," said Jack.

Li stared at Jack. "You worked with cops?"

Jack leaned against the car. "Cops on my payroll… well, the family payroll. But yeah."

"Ooh, a family payroll, did your daddy write all your checks?"

Jack chuckled at Li's jab and took a chance. "No relation, unlike you."

Li smiled. "Unlike me?"

"What can I say? Some are blessed to be royalty,"

Li chuckled. "I wish." He rubbed his eye to get the dust out of it, before cussing under his breath.

"Look, man," started Jack, seeing Li was on the fence. "I'm just a gangster on the run that heard a rumor from the bar on 5th Street that the son of a triad was locked up here, and thought if I could help him get a fresh start, he could help me."

Li looked to the sky and shook his head. "Man was I drunk." They both chuckled. Li looked at the floor apparently thinking for a moment, till he shrugged and answered, "Sure, why not."

Jack leaned his head back in surprise. "Alright, thanks!"

"No problem, on one condition, though." Li walked to Jack's stolen car.

"Anything, man."

"You buy me a six-pack and take me to my place."

"Absolutely!"

They both got in the car and drove off to the closest liquor store. Jack still flabbergasted that all it took him to get in one of the most dangerous triads in the world was a get-out-of-jail-free card and a six-pack of beer.

Chapter 3

Tour Guide

Jack parked the car in front of a less-than-five-star apartment complex. The building was dull in both color and design. Small balconies bulged out of the building, with dirty window railings. The balconies resembled the shelves of a pawn shop, each holding a different assortment of hoarded junk that no one cared to fix or was too lazy to throw away. The sidewalk leading to the complex was infested with weeds and surrounded by an uncut lawn. Overall, a decent place for someone like Li.

Jack turned off the car and asked Li, who had already opened up the six pack, why he left the Red Dragon.

"Easy. Dad found out I was a bastard son and didn't want me. Yeah, my half-siblings and I got along well, and my dad was great till he found the truth." They got out of the car and headed toward the apartment complex. "I think it was because he was starting to look at moving into politics and didn't want a bastard son messing up his image. It didn't take long till I was done with it and just left. Five years later, here I am." He stopped and stretched his arms, the six pack in one hand and a can of beer in the other. Jack chuckled at him, and they continued.

As they spoke on their way to Li's apartment, they passed a tenant with greased hair and a sleeveless shirt. Cigarette smoke followed the tenant like a priest with burning incense. Jack and Li only encountered a few other tenants on their way to the apartment. An ancient woman sat outside in the shade sucking on her dentures like a pacifier, glaring at the two of them as they walked inside.

"That's a little bit of the reason why I'm down for helping you," said Li. "It got me out of jail and a free pack of beer. If you are helpful to the Red Dragon, then awesome. But if you are a mole or something, I really don't give a damn." They walked up the stairs, Li handed Jack the six pack to free up a hand to take his keys out of his pocket, a simple looking set.

"Damn, he really burned you, didn't he?" remarked Jack.

Li chuckled. "A little, but they are still good people. I was really close to my half-siblings. To be honest, they treated me more like family than my father ever did in the end. Maybe I should go back someday." Li picked a key out of the set as they turned the corner from the stairs and walked down the hallway to the last door on the right. Jack walked behind him, observing the grungy hallway. The carpet's dark spotted pattern prevented people from seeing the dirt infesting it. The seventies style wallpaper was peeling like an invisible hand was slowly pulling it off the wall. Above Li's apartment door the fluorescent light flickered. Li's shadow cast over the doorknob as he tried to place his key in the lock. His aim was off, and he pressed the key against the knob, opening the door to his surprise. Jack set the beer down and pulled out his gun as Li stood in confusion. Jack motioned to Li to get behind him. Li slowly stepped back to let Jack lead the way, who carefully pushed the door open, letting voices out of the room.

"Where would you hide it?" one voice asked.

"In your ass," responded a second voice in an irritated tone. The rattling of drawers and doors filled the apartment as Jack walked down the entrance hall. Coming into the living room, Jack saw one of the intruders through the kitchen window checking all the empty cabinets.

Jack walked through the kitchen door and out of Li's sight. The living room was turned upside down. Li stood frozen at the sight of his small apartment ripped to pieces. His couch was torn with a knife and flipped upside down. His TV was smashed and his game console taken apart. All his framed pictures - a grand total of two - were taken apart as well, frames broken and pictures left on the floor. Li heard footsteps from his bedroom in front of him as a gasp of air came from the kitchen. A short man walked out of Li's room, wearing a sweatshirt a size too big. A handgun dangled from his hand as he looked down at a flash drive in his hand.

"Hey, look what I found," said the intruder as he looked up, meeting eyes with Li. Li ducked back into the entrance hall as the thief raised his gun towards him and fired off a quick shot that was far left. Another shot immediately followed, and Li left the apartment and would've gotten out of the building if it wasn't for Jack yelling at him.

"Li! He's down, they're all down." Jack walked out of the kitchen, wiping his fingerprints off a bloody steak knife. Dropping the knife and towel to the floor, he walked toward the bedroom. "Grab what you need, and then we leave."

Li walked back into his apartment, though he did this reluctantly as Jack searched one of the intruders laying motionless on the floor.

Jack looked at him and barked, "Get your passport and some spare clothes, now!"

Li quickly moved into his room, walking around Jack and getting a good look at the body. Li's face soured at the sight, though he had seen worse deaths, usually by knives and cleavers. Jack looked up at Li and barked again at him to get moving. Li quickly looked over his bedroom. His drawers were all pulled out with his clothes everywhere. He dropped to his knees, took his duffle bag out from under his bed, and started filling it with the clothes in his reach. He searched for his passport to no avail. His pulse sped up as he turned to give Jack the bad news. Jack was already behind him, holding his passport and searching through the invader's phone. Li snatched the passport out of Jack's hand and flipped through it, hoping it had no blood stains. It was clean.

"Look." Jack held up the phone showing a message with a picture of Li and a price under it.

Li's jaw dropped. "Just because I'm a bastard, I'm only worth a couple grand?"

Jack stood up, rolling his eyes, and wiping the phone with his shirt. He placed it back in the thief's pocket. "You got everything?"

Li checked his pockets, and double-checked his bag to make sure he had underwear. He then bent down and quickly picked up the flash drive the intruder had. Jack looked cautious at Li.

"What?" said Li. "There's some good porn on this." Li shoved the flash drive into his bag.

Jack eyed the flash drive but pushed his curiosity about it to the back of his mind and headed to the door. Li zipped up his bag with some trouble as he tried to keep up with Jack.

"So, want a guide to Hong Kong?" Li asked as he stopped to grab a beer from the six-pack before following Jack again.

"What? You don't want to die here?" Jack answered without slowing his pace down the stairs.

"Not really. But hey, seems like the best time to visit the family, see how they are all doing." They exited the building. The old lady was gone, and her chair tipped over. The street was empty. Li didn't bother with the trunk; he went directly to the passenger's seat, and placed his duffel bag on his lap. Jack accelerated the car while Li looked back to see if the police or any other unwanted people were following them. He saw and heard nothing. Jack took back alleys, one-way streets, and a sidewalk for safety. After a few minutes of that madness, Jack merged into busier roads, where they were stopped at the stop light, with a police car stopped at it as well on the other side of the street. Jack tightened his grip on the wheel and watched them out of the corner of his eye. The two cops in the car were relaxed and watching the light with few words being exchanged. As the light turned green, Jack waited for the car next to him to go first before going himself. The cops didn't even look over as they crossed the street, even with Li almost staring them down.

"So, out of curiosity, any idea who those guys were?" asked Jack, not breaking eye contact with the road.

"No clue. I don't know any people that would want me dead here. I haven't slept with any wives yet."

"What about back in Hong Kong? Any other opposing triads?"

"Yeah, but I don't see why they would want me dead?"

"The text didn't say anything about dead. Those guys could have wanted you alive." Li's eyes went wide as he processed everything. Jack thought about the flash drive.

"Maybe the Red Dragon is causing some ripples."

Jack shrugged his shoulders and said, "I don't know, maybe." He drove toward Portugal to find the first flight that would take them to the heart of the dragon.

Chapter 4

Coach

Thomas's face lit up when he saw Mathias, the little runaway he met on the Amsterdam train, across London's international airport exiting a plane with his adoptive father. Mathias's mouth didn't cease to move as he held his father's hand. Mathias's hair was longer, and he looked stronger.

"What's up with you? See a cute girl?" Li asked, looking around the area Jack was facing.

Jack chuckled. "No, just an old friend I met on a train," Jack said as he kept gazing for a moment too long as Mathias saw him across the airport. "I'll be right back," Jack said as he stood up and left Li to his phone.

"Ok, don't talk to strangers, especially cops," Li said, not looking up from his phone.

"No worries," Jack said as he walked toward Mathias, who was pointing at Thomas and almost dragging his father behind him.

"Dad, Dad! This is Thomas! He's the guy! He's the guy that helped me on the train! Nice beard!" He shook with excitement as he finally let go of his father's hand and embraced Thomas. Mathias's dad smiled as he came up behind him.

"Thomas? I've heard a lot about you. Otto Richter." Mathias's father stretched out his hand, and Thomas shook it.

"Nice to meet you. I'm glad Mathias was able to make it home."

"I am too, thank you for helping him." Otto ran his fingers through Mathias's hair. "My family owes you an enormous debt. If it wasn't for you, we would have never known what was happening and wouldn't have been able to get him out of that place and to much better places, like…?" Otto looked down at his son.

"Rugby!" Mathias said with enthusiasm.

Otto snickered. "Indeed, a lovely world we live in where I can do my business while watching rugby with my son." Otto and Mathias beamed with joy.

Thomas smiled and looked down. "It is wonderful. Sorry I didn't do more. Seeing that he made it safely takes a lot of worry off my shoulders, some guilt too."

Otto shook his head. "No need for those emotions. Your help still got him home safely, and again I am truly thankful for that."

A dull female voice boomed over the intercom, announcing the boarding of Thomas's plan.

"That's my flight, I'm going to have to go."

"Yes, we are going to have to go, too, but if you are ever in Germany, give us a call, and we will have you over for dinner." Otto drew out his business card and gave it to Thomas. Otto's name was printed nicely on the card with the law firm's name under it. "Or if you need absolutely anything, don't hesitate to call." Otto shook Thomas's hand and looked Thomas in the eyes and said with a sincere tone, "I don't think I can ever repay you for what you have done for my family, but that doesn't mean I won't try."

Mathias rushed in and gave Thomas a hug. "You're the best Thomas!"

Thomas returned the hug, trying frantically to contain the emotions rushing through his body. "No, I'm not." He whispered. They said their goodbyes and went their separate ways. Jack gained control of his emotions before reuniting with Li.

"So, how's your friend?" asked Li, still looking at his phone.

"Good, better than I thought." Jack glanced at the card again before placing it in his wallet with his fake ID and empty credit cards. Jack wondered, for a moment, if that small reunion just blew his cover. He pushed that thought out of his mind with the joy of seeing the small boy from Amsterdam safe and happy. Jack smiled again and remembered the core of this quest, for people like Mathias.

Fifteen minutes passed till they announced coach to board the plane and another fifteen minutes until Li and Jack got to their seats at the end of the aircraft. A large couple sat across the aisle from them with noise-canceling headphones on, eyes shut tight, and hands firmly grasping each other. The two seats in front of them were occupied by two older men who were already asleep before the plane even took off.

Once they were in flight, Li started to lecture Jack. "Okay, before we get to Hong Kong there are some basics you need to know."

"Ok," responded Jack. "Like what?"

"First, what do you know?" Li stared down the aisle looking for the stewardess and the food.

"Well, I know that three major triads run around Asia. The Red Dragon is the strongest and largest, followed closely by the Yellow Sun and the Gray Mountains. That's all I know."

Li nodded, still looking down the aisle before slumping back in his seat. "You know about as much as any Wiki does on the matter. But that's not a lot." Li slowly placed his focus on Jack. "Technically they aren't all triads. The Yellow Sun is a yakuza while the other two are triads because of where they all are based. Yellow Sun is from Kobe, the Grey Mountains from Shanghai, and the Red Dragon from Hong Kong." The stewardess approached them with her cart. "Finally," said Li.

Once they had gotten their food - the option of fish or fish - and drinks, they returned to their conversation with Jack asking, "So, are they structured like the European mobs?"

Li shook his head as he took a bite of his overcooked meal. "Wow, that tastes like shit. No, not really." Li forcibly swallowed. "Yes, they have a hierarchy like the western mobs, but the triads are more independent than those in the West. Have a pen?"

Jack checked his pockets for a pen to no results. Looking beside him to the larger couple, he saw a pen in the man's pocket. Jack reached over, stole it, and gave it to Li. Using his napkin, Li drew several boxes in a pyramid style. One at the top with two rows of three boxes below the first one followed lastly by two boxes at the base.

"Starting from the bottom you have your grunts called '49ers', and wannabe grunts called 'Blue Lanterns'. Moving up, you get your 'Red Poles' - they're like Capos in the European mob. Red Poles control small groups of 49ers and small areas of a city with their rackets. On the same level, you have your 'White Paper Fan', advisor to the boss, and 'Straw Sandal', the guy responsible for communication." As Li wrote down the titles in the appropriate boxes, he wrote numbers beside the headings. "Moving on up you get the 'Vanguard', 'Incense Master', and the 'Deputy'. The Vanguard finds the right Blue Lanterns, and the Incense Master is in charge of the induction ceremony for Blue Lanterns and 49ers. The Deputy is second in command to the head honcho, the 'Dragon Head', though other triads have different names for their leaders. 'Mountain Master' or 'Sun Lord' are the other names I think." Li gave Jack the pen and took the last bite of his vegetables.

"What do the numbers mean?" Jack asked as he placed the pen on the floor.

"They are like ID numbers for those positions, and - fun fact - they all start with the number four because…"

"It sounds and looks like death in Mandarin," Jack finished Li's sentence.

"Right," Li's face was unmoved by the word. Jack wondered if that would change. Worry crept into Jack's mind. He felt unsure if he would be accepted in the Red Dragon, uncertain if he would be able to climb the ranks, unsure if this insane plan would even work at granting him a glimpse at The Twelve. However, Jack was sure about one thing: death would be all around him. If this scheme was going to work, he would need to get his hands dirty - and bloody. But he felt like they already were. His train of thought was derailed as Li's phone went off.

"Alright, let's see how excited they are about our surprise visit, or how mad Dad is," Li said as he took out his cell and read the email message.

"Wait, so you have been playing the quiet game with them for how many years?" Jack asked. Li's face grew darker as his eyes moved across the screen. "What's wrong?" asked Jack.

"Dad's dead."

Chapter 5

Rain

Jack and Li stood in front of the Little Bowl, the first restaurant owned by the Lóng family. It was an older, two-story building in one of the cheaper parts of Hong Kong. The neon sign burned brightly above the canopy that covered the few tables outside. Li walked up to the door as Jack paid the cab driver. He checked his financial status and saw it was barely better than a lost dog. Jack had already burned through all his gift credit cards and most of his cash. He followed Li in, more worried about where he was going to sleep that night than his own life.

The inside was much cleaner than he had predicted. Half the red tables were occupied by an assortment of customers. The few waiters, dressed in white button-ups, lingered between tables and the pick-up window to the kitchen. A man in a sports coat and jeans stood in front of the stairs in the back corner of the restaurant. He had a concealed handgun under his jacket. Li made a straight line toward the man, ignoring everyone else as they ignored him. The man eyed him approaching. His face at first was stern but quickly changed to joy as Li got closer. They embraced each other with a hug. When Jack saw their smiles, he approached them feeling a little safer. Li introduced Jack to the man, named Yu in Cantonese. Jack lowered his eyes as he shook Yu's hand, lightly speaking in Cantonese as well. Yu raised his eyebrows.

"Your Cantonese is good, where did you learn it?" Yu asked.

"Spent a few years of my childhood in Macau" Though it may have helped that he brushed up on it the past six months he spent searching for Li. Jack knew that to help gain the trust of a man he must speak his tongue.

"Is he upstairs?" asked Li.

"Yes, and I told him you just learned about your father's death."

"Was he angry that I didn't come to the funeral?"

"No, he was trying to get a hold of you but, he had no clue where you were." Worry washed away from Li's face. Yu continued, "You all should get up there. He's been up there for an hour waiting." Yu stepped aside, and they walked up the softly lit staircase to the second floor.

Entering the second floor, Jack was surprised by how impressive it was. Half of the ceiling was glass looking up into the night sky. It slanted down before reaching behind the bar, transforming the sky and buildings of Hong Kong into a wallpaper for the room. At the other end of the chamber, six red columns stretched to the ceiling. Carved dragons crawled up each column with the most finite of details. Li and Jack walked past the guard by the stairs and went straight to the red table in the center of the room where a middle-aged man sat. He was well-dressed, his crisp black suit setting off his thin red tie and gold Rolex. Jack took note of the other guards in the corners of the room with sports coats over graphic t-shirts. A bartender stood behind the bar. Jack suspected he was also armed. When

Li reached the table, he gave his brother a warm embrace. Jack stood a couple of steps behind and waited to be acknowledged with his eyes down.

The middle-aged man scanned Jack with his dark green eyes, flawless save for the bags under them.

"I take it this is the man that bailed you out?" he asked.

Jack bowed at the waist.

Li answered for Jack. "Yes, and saved my skin. This is Jack Montferrand, Jack this is my older brother, Liao Shang Lóng or by the media for a short time Wu."

Lóng bowed his head with a chuckle. "A publicity stunt for a silly documentary. I thank you for bringing my little brother home. It is a great pleasure to have him here during this difficult time. Please have a seat." They all sat down at the round red table. The bartender brought over three identical drinks.

"So, what is this about him saving your life?"

Li filled his half-brother in on their adventure with the two thugs and their daring escape. Lóng's face was focused as he listened, as if he was studying every word Li said. Jack looked at Li every once in a while, but stared at his glass for a majority of the time, his thoughts wandering to the multiple times Jones saved him in Amsterdam. A guard behind Lóng sat down at a table while another leaned up against the wall. Once Li was finished, he gave his assumption on the matter.

"I think it was the Grey Mountains who sent them, their Mountain Master has always hated me since that one-night stand I had with his daughter."

Lóng laughed. "Damn, you almost started a war with that little stunt. Took Father a lot of money and opium to keep us at peace." Silence followed as Lóng sipped his drink. Jack did not interject anything; he only observed, his finger rubbing his glass. Li's face darkened, he took a sip of his drink and kept his eyes on it. Lóng broke the silence he started. "I don't think the Grey Mountains did it. They are under new leadership."

Li tilted his head and looked up at Lóng. "New leadership? What happened?"

Lóng said nothing as he glanced at Jack in an untrusting way.

"Don't worry about Jack, we can trust him," said Li.

"Can we?"

Jack noticed the bartender reach under the bar.

"He's killed for me, cops don't do that."

"Things have changed Li," said Lóng. "A lot has happened since you left."

Jack slowly crept his hand away from his glass and toward the edge of the table.

"I don't want to discuss them in front of a gweilo," said Lóng, using the term for 'foreign devil'. He added, a bit late, "No offense."

The bartender brought up a martini shaker and proceeded to make a martini.

"None taken," Jack answered, his body relaxing.

"I know he needs a job, and I could possibly provide one, but he will have to prove his worth, loyalty, and trust. I know it is very unlikely that they would use a gweilo as an insider to our family business. Especially because of our size at the moment."

Li frustration cooled and started to agree with his brother but was interrupted by the sound of breaking glass reverberating above their heads. It rained pieces of the broken window upon them as the sound of boots landed on the table they sat at. Jack flipped the table away with no hesitation toward the opposite direction of the exit. Jack grabbed Li by the collar and Lóng by the arm and pulled them behind the flipped table as gunshots filled the air. Jack held their heads down and ran towards the exit. The guard beside it fired frantically behind them.

"Get them out of here!" Jack ordered.

The guard grabbed them and escorted them to safety. Jack took cover behind the column next to the stairs and peeked around the corner to see what he was up against. The gunfire had ceased by this point, as there were no living guards left. He watched as the last bit of the bartender's life was beaten from him by the invader and his weapon. The attacker stood on top of the bar. He wore a pair of tired out combat boots, army black cargo pants, and a black mask that appeared to be homemade from a single piece of fabric. He was shirtless and covered in a variety of scars. He held a metal Jō staff, which was about four feet long. The assassin turned toward Jack to meet his eyes. Jack faked heading toward the exit, which he was glad he did as throwing stars hit the column he was behind and the doorpost. He heard two steps, and the invader appeared between him and the door. He was impressed by the assassin's speed, but couldn't dwell on the thought, as the invader quickly started attacking him. Jack took a defensive posture, quickly retreating and barely dodging the assassin's attacks with his Jō. After a few misses, one of his swipes hit one of the columns. Jack took his chance and placed his hand on the Jō and punched with his other hand the invader's bare stomach. His stomach was tense and hard. The assassin responded by jerking his Jō away from the column and stepping forward, twisting his Jō to catch Jack's hands and keep them from blocking his next attack, then he forcefully struck Jack's forehead with the point of his chin. Jack fell down on his back. His head throbbing and spinning like it was hit with an aluminum baseball bat, he already felt blood trickling down his face. The invader spun his Jō around his waist before carrying the momentum above his head and bringing it down straight towards Jack. Impaling the tile floor next to Jack's face, the assassin suddenly stopped and vaulted himself through the side window. A group of men appeared from the staircase with handguns drawn and opened fire over Jack at the window. They ran past Jack towards the window and scanned the alleyway.

"Did you hit him?" asked Jack, holding his bleeding forehead.

They put their guns away, and a shorter guard helped Jack up. "If we did, it didn't slow him down."

"Did you get Lóng and Li out safely?" Jack tried to regain his balance, with much difficulty. A guard brought some clean towels and ice.

"Yes, they're safe. Don't worry about them."

Yu appeared from the staircase on the phone. He stared at Jack and continued talking for a moment. He walked over and handed the cell phone to Jack with no words. Everyone was silent as Jack took it and answered.

"Jack? Lóng here. I take it you survived?"

Jack pulled back the white towel, now covered in blood, and looked around at the dead bodies in the room. One laid to his left with a throwing star deep in his throat. "More than most. Have any idea who the guy was?"

"No clue. Though I have many enemies, none of them would be crazy enough to send somebody like that."

Jack looked over one of the dead bodies. One's neck was snapped, and the jaw was in an unnatural position.

Lóng continued, "I'm thankful you were there, Jack. If it weren't for you, my brother and I would be dead right now."

"I'm glad I was able to help. Guess I've got a knack for saving Lóng's lives," said Jack, thinking that Jones would be proud.

Lóng laughed through the phone as Jack leaned against one of the columns and exchanged his bloody towel for a clean one. "You do. I hope you don't lose that skill." A short pause followed. "I know you took a big risk coming out here, looking for a fresh start, a clean slate, and after tonight I am hopeful something can be arranged. But trust is in short supply. So, the price will be high." Lóng said the last words with a menacing voice.

Jack eyed the former bartender sprawled across the bar, blood running off the bar from his head. He barely considered Lóng's next question. "Can you pay it?"

"In full," Jack answered coldly.

"I hope you will. Tomorrow morning will be your second test. Yu will drive you to your hotel room tonight and answer any questions you have. Don't disappoint."

The phone beeped as the call ended. Jack handed the phone back to Yu as the sound of sirens came from outside.

"What's my first test?" asked Jack.

"Stall them downstairs and don't get arrested," answered Yu, irritated.

Jack stumbled down the staircase to see two men in suits talking with one of the waiters in the empty restaurant. An officer stood outside.

"About time you all showed up. Even though the bastards are already gone," said Jack as he approached them, a towel still on his wound.

"And you are?" asked the taller of the two. His scruffy beard was almost unnoticeable.

"Jack Montferrand. And you?"

The shorter one scratched Jack's name on his notepad as the taller one responded. "I'm Senior Inspector Ko, and this is my partner Inspector Chiu. We are from the crime and security department. We got a call about gunshots going off."

Jack switched out his bloody towel for the waiter's towel. His bleeding had slowed down significantly. "Gunshots? It was just a brawl. The guys who started it already ran off."

Ko gestured to Chiu who closed his notepad. "Was it upstairs?"

"Yeah, but they aren't there anymore. They already ran off and are getting away." Jack pointing outside.

Ko looked at the stairs before redirecting his gaze back to Jack. "Can I at least go up there and see if everyone is alright?"

"And let them get away? What kind of inspector are you?"

"One of the best. That's why I'm going up there." Ko took a step, but Jack took a step with him.

"You aren't going up there till I get your badge number." Jack gave the bloody towel to the waiter and took his notepad and pen from the waiter's apron as he just stood there wide-eyed.

"Do you live here?" Ko folded his hands and gave Jack a hard glare as a boxer would his opponent.

"Just got here." Jack glared back, knowing he had passed the moment to act as a confused traveler and would have to be as hard as the cop to survive.

"Well, let's hope we don't see that much of each other, for your sake." Ko turned to leave with his partner and gave the officer outside no notice as they got into a non-descript car with a single rotating light on top. Jack watched as they drove off into the busy city streets. Jack threw the notepad and pen back to the waiter and took up his towel once again. Jack walked out as the last officer outside got on his motorcycle.

"Were you the one that called it in?" asked Jack as the officer placed his key into the ignition.

"I was." The officer was a young man, younger than Jack.

"Thanks, I'm glad someone at least cared about people's safety."

The officer gave a perfect smile. He looked like a stock photo of a perfect cop: short stylish hair, white teeth, and clean-shaven face. "Just doing my job sir. I'm somewhat new to the force, this being my first year, so it's encouraging to know that I'm doing it right so far."

"Really? New to the force? Are you from the area? Because I just got here today, and I'm still getting my bearings." Jack removed the towel. The bleeding had stopped, though the throbbing continued. "Know any good places this side of town to get a drink or a bite to eat that doesn't have fights?"

The officer laughed. "Well sadly I don't drink, so I can't help you there. But for places to eat: there's always a great selection of food carts at the Hong Kong Park up north that I like going to. A lot of great food for cheap."

"Cool, I know where that is. I'm Jack by the way."

"Fu," answered the officer, extending his hand. "Nice to meet you."

"Nice to meet you too. I take it you patrol this area?"

"Whenever I get a chance I do." Fu's chest puffed up slightly. "Though this is the most action I've gotten in months. Most of the time I'm doing paperwork for senior inspector Ko and working the front desk. He lets me do this patrol for a little extra cash and experience."

"Well, I don't want to get you in trouble with him. He seems like a hard fellow."

Fu chuckled. "Yeah, I suspect that's what happens when you spend so much time butting heads with the triads. Ko isn't that hard, though. I think he just enjoys fighting the triad rather than doing regular cop work. Anyway, I should get back to my patrol.

It was good talking to you. I hope to see you again." Fu placed his helmet on.

"I hope so too." They said their goodbyes. As Fu drove off into the night of the empty street, Jack said under his breath, "I hope we see each other real soon."

Chapter 6

Dragon Fire

Yu was silent for the entire drive from the hotel to their undisclosed destination. Jack asked once what he was in for, but Yu didn't answer. The ride gave Jack a good view of Hong Kong. The streets bustled with traffic in the early morning. The modern buildings shot up to the sky with a gloss on them similar to a new cell phone being taken out of the plastic. Looking back to ground level, he saw into an alleyway where a homeless man slept in a telephone booth, ignored by pedestrians and city workers. After several minutes of driving, they finally came to a halt at an old gym surrounded by a wire fence that sat at the edge of Hong Kong's business district. It seemed more like a huge, single, red brick than a building. No windows, no decor, just a door in the front and a fire escape around the corner to the second floor. Jack followed Yu out of the car and toward the gym. Yu stopped Jack, pointed to the main entrance, and said: "You take that door." His voice and movement were sober, putting Jack on his toes. Yu continued to the fire escape on the side of the gym.

"Any advice?" asked Jack.

Yu stopped at the bottom of the stairs and turned around. "Don't show weakness. We aren't like the European mobs. No favors or friends will help you through this. No cuddling, no hand-holding, no shortcuts. Just dragon fire. Don't hold back."

Yu turned around and continued up the stairs. Jack headed toward the entrance. An old faded sign saying 'Gym' hung above the door with a dragon head printed onto it, though it was barely noticeable at this hour of the morning. Jack shook all over, bouncing a bit as well.

"Go in, pass the test, climb the ranks, find The Twelve. Simple," Jack told himself before opening the heavy door and walking in.

The large gym room had a padded floor from wall to wall. Red pillars stood a few feet away from the wall, holding up a second floor balcony that encircled the gym. The second floor at the far end of the room went deeper back. Jack couldn't see well past this as his view was blocked by a line of people standing at the railing surrounding him. Jack could tell the most significant people were amassed at the far end, while the 49ers - he assumed - stood at his side. Jack saw Li standing in the middle of the onlooking crowd pointing a cell phone at him. Li smiled and gave a thumbs-up when Jack saw him. A woman in her twenties stood beside Li. Dressed in shorts and a tank top, she stood out of the crowd of casual suits, though Jack had a feeling her attire was the most expensive one there. Jack couldn't find Lóng in the group of observers. An older man stepped out from behind one of the pillars and gave Jack a pair of grappling gloves and a headpiece used in training kick-boxers. Jack, for a moment, thought the floor sounded hollow.

"Take the shoes off," the old man said in a monotone voice. Jack kicked his shoes off and started to put the gloves on. He took the headpiece and began to put it on his head, but stopped.

The old man picked up Jack's shoes with some difficulty. Jack gave the headpiece back.

The older man raised an eyebrow. "Your funeral." He took the headpiece and walked to the side and hit a giant gong. The talking settled to a mumble as Jack's opponent stepped forward onto the floor. His bald head glistened in the fluorescent light. His large, tattooed body bounced up and down as he walked toward Jack, raising his surprisingly large hands.

"You think you're tough, gweilo?"

Jack did a small bow before raising his fist. His opponent laughed. Jack stayed on his toes and slowly circled his opponent, not wanting to be cornered.

"Come on coward." He slowly extended his arm out, barely out of reach of Jack's face. He repeated the motion a few more times as Jack kept moving around him. "I hate wasting time."

The bald fighter lunged and threw a fist toward Jack's face. Jack ducked to the side and counter punched his opponent in the ear. The man stumbled away as Jack made some distance between them.

"I do too," Jack shot back, noticing his voice carrying further than he thought it would as the second floor was brought to silence.

His opponent cracked his neck and stared back at Jack with a sense of surprise before breaking out a wide grin. "There we go!"

Jack could see, out of the corner of his eye, the crowd pressing up to the railing, all eyes fixed on the both of them. Jack's opponent brought his hands up, guarding his head better, and quickly approached Jack. He backed up, then threw a leg kick. The man laughed as Jack's kick just bounced off and didn't slow him down in the slightest. Jack kept on the retreat, throwing leg kicks and light punches, all of which had no effect on his opponent's blocks. The man laughed as Jack tried to slow him down till he made his move by throwing a punch while Jack laid a heavy kick into the opponent's stomach. Jack stumbled back into a pillar. His head felt feathery as his eyebrow throbbed and blood trickled down from yesterday's wound.

His opponent laughed as he walked closer. "Good try," he said as he turned sideways and stepped his back foot in front of his front foot and used the momentum to drive his front foot toward Jack. Jack turned sideways, the heel grazed his stomach as it impacted the pillar, denting it. Before he could even pull his foot off the support, Jack landed a cross punch directly at the top of the cheekbone, followed by another punch as the opponent got his feet under him. That wasn't the end of Jack's attack: he finished it with a kick in the same spot. The opponent finally got his hands back up and his feet under him, though he had a small limp now. The bald man wiped the blood away that trickled down his face from the scar under his left eye on his cheekbone.

"Thanks," answered Jack. His opponent had stopped smiling and charged Jack with a superman punch, which Jack blocked but still felt on his face. Jack responded with a flurry of punches at his opponent's stomach, none having any effect. He backed away as his opponent threw back kicks and punches. Jack waited for an opening. It didn't take long as his opponent grew flustered at his misses. He threw wider punches and kicks that led to a wide enough opening for Jack's advantage. Jack began drilling his punches and kicks in the same spot on the face. This made the wound broader, each hit causing a puff of blood to spew out, an eerie resemblance to the men Jack shot and to Crumwell in his last moments. Jack wondered why he thought of that at this time. With each hit the blood poured even faster as his flashbacks became more vivid, until his opponent finally landed one of his shots in Jack's rib cage. Before Jack could stumble back to catch his breath, the bald man grabbed his head. The left side of his face was mostly clean. Blood covered below his right eye. Jack focused on keeping himself from throwing up while his opponent mocked him.

"Nice try Lumberjack." He pulled Jack's head up as he brought his leg back to knee him in the face. Jack quickly clenched his opponent's head, jerking it side to side to prevent his opponent the stance and control to knee Jack. Before the man got his feet back under him, Jack pulled the bald head down sharply into his rising knee. His opponent went limp on the floor.

Jack bent over, hands on knees. Sweat fell from his face, along with blood. He breathed out and said, "Thanks for the name."

Li quickly broke the silence, giving a loud cheer and raising his empty hand. Though all the other faces were wide-eyed in shock, the girl beside Li had no change in her expression. She snapped her fingers twice, and without a missed beat six men climbed over the railing and jumped down to Jack's level, surrounding him. Jack moved to the first one that hit the floor, landing a few solid blows as he tried to recover from the fall. Jack turned to the other five as the sixth was out of the fight for the moment. They attacked all at once. Throwing crowded kicks and punches as Jack kept moving back to the wall under Li to prevent being surrounded. Jack attempted to redirect as many of the attacks as he could while trying to respond to any openings. A few of his offenses hit their mark: throat, neck, and crotch. When three were taken down by this tactic, Jack started to move again so as to keep only one opponent in front of him. That didn't work too well as the shortest one of them sprinted around and did a flying kick into Jack's shoulder. Jack sneered in pain but quickly grabbed the kicker's hair and punched him. He pulled the kicker into a headlock and used his small body as a human shield, laying a punch into his shield to keep him in submission. Jack backed to a pillar and threw the barely conscious boy into another fighter and tackled a separate opponent, dazzling him as his head hit the mat. Jack rolled over the opponent's head and struck him with a hammer fist as he stood up. The last two fighters stood at a distance for a moment, for once wary of going on. The gong rang, and the last standing fighters relaxed and sat down, breathing heavily and wincing in pain. Jack finally observed the carnage for the first time. Blood spatter covered all of his opponent's dress shirts.

The older man came up to Jack's side with his shoes, his face unchanged but his eyes a little wider. "Showers are over there." He pointed to a door behind Jack.

Jack took his shoes and walked to the unmarked door. As he turned, he saw a glimpse of the onlookers. Their expression mostly unchanged since he landed the first punch. Raised eyebrows and watchful eyes observed his every movement, except for the smiling Li and the girl, who was biting her lip.

Chapter 7

Secure Towels

Jack kept the shower on as he slowly undressed. Once he was down to his undergarments, he looked at himself in the fogging sink mirror. Dark blue and purple bruises covered his body from the shoulders down. His right shoulder had bulged up with blood and was hot to his touch. The rest of the bruises were on his torso, with a few on his legs. His swollen eyebrow had started bleeding out at the corner. He removed the small bandage on his forehead to see if it was bleeding again. It was. He slowly felt around the injuries on his torso to see if he had any broken ribs, which he didn't think he had. He held his breath and stroked his ribs like a piano. He released a sigh of relief as his assumption was correct. Jack could barely see himself in the mirror as steam filled the entire bathroom and escaped through the door less entryway.

"Dude, you look like you just got out of a meat grinder." Li stood at the entrance of the bathroom staring at him with a hint of pain on his face.

Jack tilted his head and looked down on Li like a parent with a sassy child. Li didn't recognize that as his face flipped to excitement. "But, you did it! You survived the Dragon Fire!"

"Surviving and thriving are two different things. I take it I did well?" Jack asked as he stripped down and entered the shower, washing the blood off his body.

"Starting off at the second tier helped you a bit and taking him down that fast. Incredible! Most guys don't get past him at all." Li sat on the wooden bench attached to the wall.

"What did Lóng think?" Jack asked.

Li snorted at the question. "He was impressed like everyone else."

"That's good. Who was the girl beside you?" Jack turned off the shower and dried himself with a towel.

"Lei Lei, my half-sister."

Jack chuckled, which morphed into a sneer of pain. "Damn, that hurts."

Li laughed. Jack came out of the shower with a well-secured towel around his waist. He held another towel over his cuts. "That's not even the best part," said Li, with a sense of pride. "You're the second one to finish it all without being knocked out."

Jack placed new bandages over his cuts. "Well, knowing now that I made a great impression, what's next?"

"I'm not sure, I think Lóng has an errand for you before you can become a 49er."

Jack looked at Li, a band-aid in his hand. "A 49er already?"

"Yeah. I don't know all the details, but things aren't great. But it may help us both."

"I'm okay with that. Do you know what kind of errand?"

Li shrugged.

"What do you know, just out of curiosity?"

Li laughed. "I know Lóng still has trust issues, I'm still not sure he trusts me entirely." As Li said this, his bright face faded away.

"Why wouldn't he trust you?" asked Jack.

"Just the times I guess." Li looked down at his hands. "Heard the transition of leadership was hard if it wasn't for his mom. That's why I'm glad he likes you so far. It's personally helping me out again."

"Why?" Jack finished bandaging himself up. "I mean, you had the chance to just ask me to drop you off someplace where you could hit the road again, be your own man, and stay out of 'the clutches of the Red Dragon' as you put it. But your instinct was to come back. Why?"

Li looked up, his head atilt. "I don't know, man. I mean, I guess I thought I would be safer here, but they aren't a charity case. Even when my dad was in charge, everyone had to earn their place and… if it wasn't for my stepmom I wouldn't have gotten nearly as far as I did while he gave Lóng the moon and Lei Lei the sun. I didn't want to have to go up against that at the time." Li rubbed his hands together. His jaw tensed.

"Hey," Jack said. Li looked up at him. "We will earn our place here. We are going to make this our home."

Li smiled with a hint of sympathy. "I hope you pass, man," he said. "I really need a friend I can trust."

Jack felt a pang of guilt.

Chapter 8

A Mole After a Mole

"It's not much, but it will make do for our situation," said Yu, turning on the lights to his small apartment. A folded-up card table leant against the wall next to the dirty kitchen. "I know the couch doesn't look like much, but it's comfortable." The couch was brown, and Jack couldn't tell if it was from the fabric or the dirt. It sat in the middle of the living room in front of a new curved LED TV. Behind the couch was a glass door to a balcony big enough for only two people standing.

"Not too shabby," lied Jack as he stepped onto the stained carpet.

"I like it. Want a beer?" asked Yu from the kitchen.

"Sure. So, what's the job Lóng wants me to do?"

Yu returned and handed Jack a Sapporo beer. "The Dragon Head wants you to find the undercover cop that ratted us out so he can deal with him," Yu said, emphasizing Lóng's position and not missing a beat.

"Where do I start?" Jack said, not missing a beat either.

"We don't know. We had some guys looking for him, but they kept coming up empty-handed. Now they will be busy watching Lóng and finding the bastard assassin from yesterday." Yu plopped himself down on the couch. Jack walked behind the sofa to look out the balcony onto Hong Kong. Yu added, "Since you did such a great job finding Li, this shouldn't be any harder."

"Yeah, but Li wasn't in protective custody. I bet this guy is."

"Yes, but we have some stuff you can work off of." Yu pulled out a folded piece of paper from his pocket and handed it to Jack. "This is all the info I have. Basically, he is from our Chinese division. Surprisingly, they placed him in Hong Kong. There is also a picture of him when he worked for us about four years ago."

Jack read the paper but found nothing useful other than the picture and his habits of clubbing.

"So, can you find him in two weeks?"

"It will take some luck," said Jack, "but yeah, I can find him. I'll need to make some new friends first."

Chapter 9

Smile

Officer Fu walked into Inspector Ko's office with a folder in one hand and a cup of tea in the other. He placed both of them on the Inspector's desk as Ko hung up the phone.

"Here's your tea and my report from the night at the Little Bowl."

Ko took a sip of his drink, smacking his lips and scrunching his face. "Took you long enough."

"Sorry, sir." Fu lowered his head, though the incident happened only a few days ago.

Ko looked up from the report to Fu, who was still standing in Ko's cluttered office. "Anything else?" Ko asked, annoyance in his voice.

"Uh, yes," Fu said. "Out of curiosity, why didn't you check upstairs?"

"It would have been a waste of time." Ko went back to the report.

"Why?"

"Because," Ko said, not even looking up. "That gweilo kept us delayed too long. The triad would have been cleaning that up as they were shooting them. Also, I don't waste my time with bar fights."

"How did you know it wasn't them?" said Fu generally curious.

"Because," Ko closed the report roughly, "you don't catch the triad off their feet. You aren't lucky with them. You have to be ahead of them. Also, the triad doesn't use guns unless it's absolutely necessary." Ko handed the report back to Fu. "The report's a bit long and lazy, but it will do."

Fu took the report and opened his mouth for another question, but Ko cut him off. "And no, you can't have more patrol time."

Fu left Ko's office, gingerly closing the door behind him. The police station's low buzz filled the air with white noise. Fu walked through the light bustle of cops towards the front desk, his desk, a place filled with papers, an ancient computer, and a single picture of his young wife holding an ultrasound of his first child, who he hoped was still well. He sat himself down and pushed his disappointment to the back of his mind and a smile to the front of his face that could fool even himself.

Unnoticed to Fu, someone did see through the smile - because he had worn it himself for the past six months. Jack took a moment longer blankly staring at Fu as he thought of the long days he had to wear that smile, that fake smile, the façade that everything was alright, though the memory of Mallory still ate Jack up at night. He took a breath to regain his thoughts before approaching Fu with his own fake smile.

"I didn't know you worked here?"

Fu looked up to see the familiar face he met two nights ago. "Hey Jack, yeah this is my station. Your head looks better."

Jack touched the two small band-aids that covered his wound. He was cautious not to smear the makeup over his other cut.

"Thanks, it wasn't as deep as I thought it was, luckily."

"That's good. So, what can I help you with?" Fu gave Jack his full attention.

Jack rested his arms on the front desk to say, "Well, I seem to have misplaced a friend."

"That's not good."

Jack continued before Fu could reach down to get the missing person paperwork. "It's not like a missing person thing, I just don't know what name he is using nowadays."

Fu raised an eyebrow. "Nowadays?"

Jack chuckled and wondered if it was convincing enough. "See, I knew him before he moved to Hong Kong when he had a small gambling problem. So, he created, I guess you could say, a habit of changing his name when he got into too much debt. Anyway, he told me he was moving here last time I saw him and gave me a number so I could get a hold of him but…"

"The number doesn't work?" said Fu, filling in the missing pieces.

"You got it. And I know he'd changed his name at least a couple of times before this. So…"

"You would like me to help you find him?" Fu filled in the pieces again.

Jack's face lit up. "Yes. If you can? I really want to get him some help, because as you can probably tell, it's a problem."

Fu laughed. "It seems like it. I would be honored to help, but I need something to go off of."

Jack held up a finger and reached into his pocket, pulling out a photo of a young man of Chinese descent and a name. "He may not look just like that, hair and beard could be different.

Does that help? To be honest, with his habit, I'm not sure if he's alright."

Fu looked over the picture then up at Jack. His face worried. Fu cracked a smile. "Sure, I can help you find him. Can't promise more than a working number, though. Security stuff."

Jack smiled and nodded. "Totally understandable,"

"Well, give me a day. Where I can reach you?" Fu took out a Post-it Note and a pen.

"Well, I don't have a phone yet, so how about we meet at the market you were talking about tomorrow for lunch? My treat."

"Sure, we will meet where all the food carts are. You can't miss it." Fu wrote it down and placed it on the photo. "I'm always down for a free meal."

Chapter 10

Extra Hours

Officer Fu sat quietly at the front desk as his twelve-hour shift neared a close. He was one of a few officers left in the station. They were all working with their patrol partners. It was a quiet evening for their sector of Hong Kong. Fu was checking the time when Inspector Ko walked in front of his desk.

"I'm gone. If anything comes up triad-related, give me a call."

Fu looked up confused. "Sir, I'm about to clock out, if you want…"

Ko cut Fu off with an irritated sigh and stopped in his tracks halfway toward the door and turned around. "No, you're not clocking out. You said you wanted more time; I'm giving it to you."

"I was asking for patrol hours, sir."

"Then walk around your desk if you want to patrol something." Ko turned back toward the exit.

"Sir, I do have one more question about…"

Ko stopped at the door with one hand on it and turned around again. "I don't know what they taught you at the academy, but here at the heart of Hong Kong, at this low-life station, I give orders. You take them. That's it. If I hear one more question from you, I'll take your badge. Do I make myself clear?"

Fu nodded, his eyes facing the floor. Ko left the building.

"Sorry about that," said Officer Cho a few desks behind Fu as he packed up his things to go home. "Ko can be a bitch. Even my dad had difficulty with him, but he's talented and will be there when the chips are down."

Fu kept staring at the floor in the direction of Cho. "It's alright. I don't remember Ko being that angry when I first started a few months back."

"Didn't you hear? Funding for the anti-organized crime section got the biggest cut a few days ago. They are underfunded and undermanned at the moment." Cho packed his things and started toward the door but stopped in front of Fu's desk first. "Ko once had an office at the Central Government Complex before his demotion with a few other men and my dad."

"He was demoted?"

"Yeah, he took a pay cut, demotion, and an office move all for the 'cause'. The problem is you still need the people upstairs for support, and right now they don't see the triad as a threat. That department is probably running on a fourth of what they were."

"So, they don't want him doing any triad stuff?"

Cho snapped his fingers. "Yep, unless it falls into his lap. And even then, it would probably end up being taken from him and passed up the chain. Anyway, I have to go, but keep your spirit up. The longer you are here and the older you get, the more respect he will start having for you. Goodnight."

Officer Fu thanked him. Officer Cho tapped the desk and left the station, telling him not to mention it. Fu opened his drawer and picked up his cell phone and texted his wife that he wouldn't make it home for dinner… again. Fu placed the phone on his desk and closed the drawer but not before noticing the picture with the Post-it Note on it. He took the picture out and rolled over to the fax machine to scan it into his computer. He breathed slowly trying to ease his frustration at his superior. Fu had been with Ko for almost half a year now, since graduating from the academy, and hadn't heard a single positive thing from him. The scan finished. His phone buzzed. He rolled back to the desk and opened his phone before his computer. His wife had asked if he could still pick up her newest prescription. He agreed, of course, and asked how she was feeling. He thought through the drug stores that would still be open as he opened up the database and the cost of her new prescription. The computer searched most of the people in Hong Kong, though some were still not in the system due to its relatively newness. A denied access screen popped up asking for a login name and password. He typed in Ko's name and password. Fu was almost Ko's personal secretary, so he knew the password naturally as Ko kept it on a note beside his desk. His cell phone buzzed again. She'd sent a single emoji with a medical mask. He sent back an emoji with a single tear.

"This doesn't pay enough," he whispered to himself. He looked at the loaded results. Fu leaned forward, surprised that the system was able to find Jack's friend. That was soon dwarfed by what else he found.

Chapter 11

Pork Buns

Jack was observing an older merchant selling fish to an older group of ladies when Fu found him.

"Hey Jack, how are you?"

Fu's face looked like a perfect picture. Jack hoped that it would stay that way.

"Better that you are here. Were you able to find my friend?"

Fu's smile remained, but his eyes narrowed. Jack's muscles tightened. "Yeah, but it's complicated."

Jack watched Fu's movements as he stood still in civilian clothes. Jack glanced behind Fu. "What kind of complicated?"

"Let's find a place to eat, and I'll explain."

They found a place further into the market at Fu's suggestion, with no objections from Jack. It was a small vendor who had set a few cheap, two-seat tables and chairs near his cart to portray the sense of a brick and mortar restaurant. The middle-aged owner only offered three variations of steamed pork buns. As they waited to order they talked about small things. Fu seemed to ask a lot of the personal questions toward Jack, which Jack tried to return to him, but Fu kept his answers short. After they had ordered, they sat at a table away from the busy street. Looking behind Fu, Jack could still see the old man bartering with the group of ladies, mainly with the youngest one as the other two seemed to have lost interest.

"That's a good Cha Siu Bao! How's yours?" asked Officer Fu with a mouth half full.

"Amazing, though it may be better if I knew what this mysterious complication is?" His voice quivered for a second. He hoped Fu didn't notice. Fu had already taken another bite. "Don't tell me he's in prison?" Jack asked in a sarcastic voice to cover up his earlier vocal mistake.

Fu chuckled. "Not in prison." Fu's voice quickly changed to a serious tone. "Protective custody."

Jack wasn't surprised by this but made out to be. "What? Why?"

"I can't tell you, to be honest. I've already said too much." Fu took a bite of his pork bun, as if he wanted a reason not to talk.

"Can you at least tell me he's alright?"

Fu shook his head, his shoulders hunched, eyes on food. Out of the corner of Jack's eye, he saw the two older ladies leave the old man selling raw fish, though the man kept aggressively bartering with the younger woman. Jack knew he would have to take a risk.

"Why not? Don't you trust me?"

Fu's face frowned in guilt. "It's not that I don't trust you," Fu said. "It's where and when I met you that is questionable."

Jack widened his eyes. "Is it because I'm an American? A gweilo?"

Fu almost dropped his pork bun. "No! Not at all! The restaurant we met at is rumored to be backed by triad members, and I don't want to put you in a dangerous position."

"Ok," said Jack, rethinking his tactics. "Let's assume your fears of me are true," started Jack. "That is at the core of it: the fear that I'm a triad member. If that's true you would report it to your superior, bring a gun, a badge, and some other officers to arrest me when I give any hint of triad involvement or illegal stuff."

Fu stopped chewing.

"However," continued Jack, "you didn't bring a gun or any undercover cops. I bet you didn't even tell anyone where or what you were doing for lunch." Jack stole a glance at the young lady standing silently looking at the fish the older man was holding as if he had made his final case in their bargaining. Jack made his own final case. "Which means, you are open to the idea of telling me. Am I wrong?"

Fu swallowed and opened his mouth to respond but was interrupted again by a child who appeared from the busy street. The little girl's hair was in small pigtails that bounced as she approached their table, eyeing their food. Jack watched Officer Fu as he switched gears and talked to the child with a bright smile on his face. The girl ignored him and started to reach for his food before her mother pulled her away. The mother apologized. Fu took no offense and stayed kind and friendly. Showing no sign of the type of talk he had moments before, Jack held a similar face as Fu and watched the scenario play out. After the mother and the daughter left, Fu returned his attention to Jack, face still smiling. Jack smiled in return, pulled out a folded envelope, and slid it to the middle of the small table.

"I hear," said Jack, "that whatever stress the husband has, the wife will have. And whatever stress the wife has, the baby will have."

Fu focused his gaze on Jack, his smile replaced by aggression. Jack watched the daughter and mother walk further away then continued, "And let's face it, it is harder to be stressed when the bills are paid, the doctor is the best, your pockets are full, and you're home on time."

Fu's jaw kept tight, but his eyes softened as he looked down at the envelope and whispered, "I don't want her…Mallory…to be in on this at all."

Mallory? Jack blinked once to gain composure. He wasn't sure Fu had said Mallory or if grief was deciding what he was hearing. Glass had trained Thomas to play a part. They hadn't warned him that the past would play him.

"They won't," Jack said. "No member will come near them, no information given. They will never know. All they will know is that you are a husband that supports them substantially."

Fu took the envelope, his face gentler. He slowly opened it and looked at the contents of it. He closed the envelope and his eyes for a moment. The old man was wrapping the fish up as the young lady was paying, smiles on both faces, a successful transaction. The mother and the daughter walked by the sale.

"I want the best doctors helping her," said Fu as he glared at Jack with threatening eyes, a storm brewing behind them.

"The best and the brightest know nothing about me," replied Jack.

The storm settled a bit behind Fu's eyes. He reached into his pocket, pulled out the picture. He took out a pen and wrote down an address on the back of it and handed it to Jack, who folded it up and placed it in his pocket.

"I'll keep in touch with you only," said Jack. "Don't worry about when or where. I'll take care of that. If you need to get a hold of me, use a payphone and this number." Jack wrote a number down on a napkin. "Just keep doing what you're doing with that perfect smile, and you will start to feel that stress fly away, as well as the stress of your family."

Jack stood and began to walk away but stopped behind Fu with one last thing. "I appreciate you for doing this, and I will continue to show my appreciation." Jack left Fu to his thoughts and his new 'bonus.'

Chapter 12

The Line

Jack tried to keep track of how many turns and how long of a distance between the turns as he was driven blindfolded to meet Lóng, the Dragon Head of the Red Dragon. After twenty minutes of driving and more than twenty turns and several stops, Jack gave up on trying to know where he was going. Once the car stopped and the engine turned off, Jack's face was uncovered to a parking garage. Yu opened the car door as the other guard beside him went to the trunk to retrieve the unconscious mole. Jack helped the guard carry the bound man to the elevator with Yu leading the way. As they waited for the elevator, Jack tried to get a hint of where he was by his surrounding. The garage had only a few cars, and the ones it did have looked as if they'd just driven off the lot. The elevator arrived with a ding. They entered and rode it to the twelfth floor. Yu asked Jack why he was chuckling.

"My ex lived on the twelfth floor. I find it a little ironic."

The doors opened to an empty floor that resembled a hotel floor. Two guards stood outside the third door on the right. They were well dressed and armed. One of them gave a knock as he saw them coming and opened the door slightly, saying something through the crack. Once the three men and their unconscious baggage were there, the guard opened the door for them, and they all walked in.

Lóng and his half-brother Li were seated on a couch in the living room, waiting. Their tea sat on the glass coffee table above a white rug. Lóng's face was pleasantly surprised while Li gave a smug look of pride as they placed the middle-aged man on the wood floor next to the carpet.

"I'm impressed. Four days early," said Lóng.

"I told you he was good," commented Li proudly.

Lóng ignored him and stood up, keeping his eyes on the mole like a cat on a rat. "How did you do it?" he asked.

"Made a friend who had access to some police files and I compensated him for it."

"That explains why you wanted that cash," Yu interjected.

"I told you I would pay you back," said Jack.

Lóng picked up his drink and interrupted. "Don't worry Yu, you will get your money back. And Jack, we will have a conversation tomorrow about this 'friend,' but for right now I want to have some alone time with this old friend."

Lóng poured his drink on the mole's face. The mole awoke, shaking his head and trying to move his arms and legs. The struggle lasted only a few seconds as his eyes opened and they met Lóng's. His breathing quickened as the Dragon Head bent down closer. "Good evening. I hope you slept well," Lóng said.

The mole tried to reply through his duct-taped mouth to no avail. "If I weren't in my position," said Lóng, "I would be impressed by your accomplishment in China. However, I am in my position, and you are in yours."

Tears started to make their way out of the man's eyes.

"It's a little late for that," said Lóng as he wiped the tears away. "Take him to the kitchen; I will be there shortly."

The man let out a muffled scream as two other guards appeared from the entrance hall behind Jack and picked up the scrambling mole and carried him through a door to the right. Lóng stood up and approached Jack. "Li has spoken highly of you, and now I'm starting to see some good reasons. Li will help you through the rituals while I deal with my old friend. I hope you like tattoos."

Lóng left through the same door the mole went. Li slapped Jack's back and congratulated him, though Jack wasn't fully there as he heard the mole plead for his life from the kitchen, begging to be permitted to call his wife to hear her voice one last time. Li guided Jack to the door. Jack was able to finally step away from the situation and come to realize his hands were getting dirtier. Jack wondered what happened to Thomas Thornhill. Thomas wouldn't have killed so easily. He was becoming more Jack Montferrand and less Thomas Thornhill, and he didn't like it. Mallory wouldn't have liked it either.

"You did it!" said Li with relief in his voice. "No one can question your trust now. Hey, you okay?" asked Li.

"Yeah," Jack said. Thomas would have said 'no.' "Just enjoying this moment of my new life."

Jack showed no sign of what stirred in his mind as he walked out. He didn't miss a step as Li explained and joked about the ritual that Jack was about to partake in. Jack felt like he, as Thomas Thornhill, was awaking from a trance. The screams pulled Thomas into third person, and he honestly started thinking about what he had just done as Jack. The man's muffled pleas echoed in his mind as similar to what Thomas imagined the home base sounded like. Was that but six months ago? Six months ago everyone at base was still alive. This was now only Thomas's dreams, to hear Mallory's voice one last time. He wondered how this was any different from the killers and criminals he had slaughtered with his hands before. He had killed more than a dozen men who tried to stab him, shoot him, or strangle him. Thomas Thornhill wondered on the difference, but Jack Montferrand lived the difference. The man he brought to Lóng to be killed was just another step to The Twelve. Jack threw the answer to the back of his mind, and he leaned back in the car, traveling with Li to visit the Incense Master.

Jack tried to engage the moment as he listened and followed the Incense Master's instructions. Jack said the oaths and cut the ceremonial pig. But after it was all said and done and he stood there a full-fledged 49er of the Red Dragon, he could still hear the answer. Thomas tried responding to the screams, thinking of the lives that wouldn't be destroyed once he got to the top of the Red Dragon and found The Twelve. But they persisted, growing louder in his head, louder than the screams, all echoing in Mallory's voice. Innocent or not, the mole didn't deserve that kind of death. He was simply a man fighting for a better world, a man exposing the truth, a man trying to live a peaceful life with his family before Jack ended it. He was a man just like Thomas. Thomas had killed himself. Jack agreed to Li's idea of going to a club to celebrate. If he couldn't avoid the screams, he would drown them out in noise and liquor.

Chapter 13

Rookie

Everyone's idea of a celebration is different. Jack's idea was the polar opposite of Li's. Though Jack wouldn't consider this a celebration, he knew it was a success in some way of getting closer to The Twelve. The cab he rode in with Li pulled up to a club called 'The Boom' which was as loud as it sounded. Club music pounded at Jack's eardrums as they entered the dark dance floor. The ground changed colors, as did the spotlights above, with the beat of the music. Li started to explain something about the club until he saw twins dancing with each other. Before Jack knew it, Li had disappeared onto the dance floor after them.

Jack took a breath; he finally had a moment to himself. Being almost a head taller than everyone else, he scanned the club easily. The other side of the dance floor had karaoke rooms filled with happy, tipsy people singing pop songs from around the world. At the end of the club was a bar, double stacked with people waiting for their drinks. Seeing most of the bartenders were men, Jack assumed he would have to wait until morning to get his drink. Right above the bar was a balcony enclosed in glass that looked over the dance floor. The atmosphere of the second floor appeared expensive and blessedly quieter than the first floor. He immediately looked for a way to get up there. It didn't take long. He located the stairs near the bar, back in the corner, a guard in front. As Jack made his way there, he saw Li dancing with the twins and motioning toward him to join them. Jack smiled and pointed toward the balcony with an open hand. Li nodded. Jack reached the guard, who asked for his name. After giving it, the guard let him through and said, "Welcome to the family."

A calmness settled into him as the absence of sound filled his ears. The back wall of the second floor was deeper than Jack had thought and was mostly taken up by a yet another bar with colored lights shining up through the hundred bottles. Three bartenders tended it as the guests talked in their small groups standing near the window or sitting on silver chairs that surrounded little glass tables. This fit Jack's idea of a celebration much better. Jack approached an occupied area of the bar where a black bartender with an afro attended him as soon as he sat down.

"Good evening, sir. How are you tonight?" asked the bartender in a chipper yet calm voice.

Jack let out a tired sigh. "I'm alright,"

"Doesn't sound like it, girl trouble?" the bartender asked sincerely. The first time anyone asked him a sincere question in a while.

"No. Guilt trouble." Jack himself was taken aback by what he said.

The bartender stopped from reaching a bottle on the top shelf and opened a cabinet under the bar. "I guess you're the new 49er then?"

Jack's ears perked up. "49ers? Like the football team?"

The bartender chuckled as he placed three bottles on the bar and proceeded to mix a drink for Jack. "You don't have to play dumb. Lóng owns the place and I'm an old friend of Li. He told me about you yesterday. Jack, if I'm correct?"

"Yeah, and you are?"

"Saul and this, Jack, should help you relax a bit." Saul placed an orange slice in the drink and a large ice cube on the orange slice which kept it pinned to the bottom of the short glass. Jack took a sip and was flabbergasted by the taste.

"Now that hits the spot! What is it?" He took another sip,

Saul placed the bottles and other items away. "My own concoction. I call it the Rookie. I give it to all the new 49ers who come up here. It helps them through it."

"So, you know what I went through?" Jack asked softly.

Saul made a glance down the bar. The customers at the bar all had a drink and were talking among themselves. Saul returned his attention to Jack. "I know more than an internet search. You should be aware by now the Red Dragon has a lot of trust issues at the moment. Whenever they get new blood, they have to be certain beyond a shadow of a doubt that the rookie isn't a mole… certain by any means necessary. Through innocent blood, moles are ratted out."

Jack swirled the ice cube around in his glass softly. "I mean, it's smart." Fire and blood started to fill his mind again.

Saul straightened up as if an idea had hit him. "What you need is a friendly conversation not related to triad affairs to get your mind off of it."

"I thought that's what this is for?" Jack held up his almost empty glass, a little bit of him hoping Saul would make him another.

Saul scoffed. "I told you it would help you relax, not forget it. Alcohol is the worst for taking care of guilt. Conversations with beautiful women with just a bit of alcohol will help you forget."

Jack shook his head while lowering his glass back to the bar. "I'm not really in the mood for sex."

Saul gave a short laugh. "I know. If you were, you wouldn't be here." Saul glanced around for a conversation partner.

"I'm not even sure I'm in the mood to talk to a girl."

Saul looked back at Jack with a raised eyebrow. "Oh? Still getting over the last one?"

Jack remembered the hard way how personal questions in Hong Kong could get. "Sort of, it was a really bad breakup."

Saul made a painful sigh. "Breakups are the worst, but hey. Better now than five years into a marriage."

Jack nodded in agreement while finishing off his drink. Mallory's office space covered in ash and blood invaded his mind.

Saul brought out a few different bottles and made Jack another drink. "I'm saying all this stuff to show you it could be worse." He placed two pink colored glasses in front of Jack. "But, in the end, it still sucks even when you try to move on. It gets better in the long run. So, how about a fun talk?"

Jack looked at the two glasses. He wondered what Mallory would say, what her input would be. She never did like it when he was sad and did whatever she could to bring him out of his little funks.

"I don't see how it would hurt," Jack murmured.

Saul took one of the glasses and tapped the bar. "Stay here." Saul almost started to walk away, but Jack stopped him.

"Why are you doing this?"

Saul put the drink back down but didn't take his hand off of it. He looked at Jack dead in the eye with a sympathetic smile. "Because I was once in your shoes. I had been through some shit, done some shit that I'm not proud of, ran here to get away from it all, found myself alone with no friends, people just staring at me because of obvious reasons, and a bunch of guilt digging at my soul. I was, no lie, one terrible day from hanging myself, and I had a lot of terrible days. But then I met Mr. Lóng, Li's father, and everything changed. And I will tell you rest of it later, but first I want you to meet someone."

Saul left with one of the drinks and approached a group of girls already dispersing, except for one who was checking her phone. Saul exchanged words with her, nodded toward Jack, and handed her the drink. The girl placed her phone away and walked over to Jack. Her attire was of one who knew how to dress. She wore a pink sundress that was quite modest compared to the rest of the dresses in the club. As she walked, her short hair bobbed, revealing her ears and the several small earrings she had.

She stopped next to Jack and asked in perfect English, "I hear you're an American?"

Jack smiled in relief. "It's so nice to hear English. Yes, I am. I take it you are as well?"

She smiled and took a seat beside him, not taking her attention off him. "Yes. My father was an American, and my mother was Vietnamese. So, I spent a lot of time in America." Her voice was energetic. Her hands made small movements as she spoke. "My name is Amy, by the way." She reached her hand out. Jack shook it, her hands soft to his touch.

"Nice to meet you, Amy. My name is Jack. So, how did your parents meet?"

"My father was a pilot, and my mother was a stewardess. They met on one of his international flights."

"That's cool." Jack took a sip of his new drink. It was much lighter than his first, but still delicious.

"I know, I've been trying to get my father to write it all down, but he's always putting it off. But what about you?" she asked with a tilt of her head.

"What about me?" Jack repeated with a small chuckle. She laughed in return. Jack's eyes brightened up.

"Yeah, sorry," Amy said. "How did you end up in Hong Kong? Traveling through and wanted to see the nightlife?"

"No," said Jack. "I just moved here. Doing some contract work around the city, freelance stuff. What about you?"

Amy smiled. "What about me?"

They both laughed. "Kidding," she said, "I'm an interior designer at an architect firm. I moved here after I graduated from NYU and did a couple of internships around the city before finally getting hired for a full-time position."

"Wow, that's amazing."

The balcony lounge emptied of old customers, filled with new, and emptied again until all that was left was Jack and Amy with a few employees. They had talked the night and part of the morning away about a wide variety of things, from favorite bands and books to embarrassing childhood stories and arguing over the best children's cartoon. Amy finally departed after she saw the time, leaving Jack in a much better state than he arrived in. Saul came up to him with his jacket on.

"How are you doing now?"

Jack reached for his wallet and smiled. "A lot better, how do you know her?" Jack handed Saul the last bit of cash he had for the drinks.

"Don't worry about the drinks," said Saul. "49ers get a free pass their first night."

Jack was inwardly relieved as he put his money back in his empty wallet.

"She comes here every once in awhile," said Saul. "She's very easy to talk to, so it was easy for us to become friends. I always see at least one or two guys hit on her, but she hates fake people."

Saul and Jack walked out together, passing the janitors cleaning up the trash and mopping the floors.

"I'm not surprised by that," said Jack. "Thanks for sending her my way. The talk was helpful."

"Don't think of it."

A few lone cars drove past them as they exited the building. The only light came from the signs and street lamps. Buildings hid the moon, and man-made lights swallowed up the moonbeams.

"Well, it was fun to talk to you, Jack." Saul shook Jack's hand.

"It was my pleasure, Saul. Hope to see you again soon and hear the rest of that story."

"Oh, you will. Be careful out there, Jack. Though, I think you already know that."

The corner of Jack's mouth smiled. "Yeah, sort of. This isn't my first time with organized crime."

"I wasn't talking about that."

Jack's small smile faded. "The last thing I want is a girl in my life at this moment."

Saul nodded, his face understanding. "I know. You're a smart guy thinking that way. Just try not to fall too hard for her, okay? Guys have a tendency to do that."

"I'm not surprised. I hate to disappoint, but I won't be one of those guys."

"Sure," Saul said sarcastically.

They laughed and went their separate ways. Jack hoped Saul's prediction was wrong. Guilt knocked at the corner of his mind as he thought for a moment about Amy, guilt that came not from murder, but from cheating.

Chapter 14

Daughter of a Dragon

Jack was still drowsy as he followed Yu up the back stairs of the gym. The upper room looking over the gym floor was similar to a lounge. It had a pool table, a dartboard, and a refrigerator next to the counter. The Incense Master, a man by the name of Ink, sat next to the railing, watching a few young 49ers sparring. He was in his late seventies. His hairless skin seemed to drape over his bones. His tattoos dropped with it. A black bag sat beside him. Yu stopped at the pool table and tapped on it.

"Take your shirt off," Yu told Jack.

Jack obeyed and sat on the pool table while Ink stood up with his black bag and walked over. Jack watched Ink opened his bag and brought out a tattoo needle and ink.

"Nice to see you again," said Jack trying to start up a conversation. Ink said nothing tapping on the table. "Is this part of the initiation?" Jack asked as he laid chest down on the pool table. Yu shook his head.

"Used to be optional, but Lóng wants every new 49er to have one."

"Do I get an option on what it is?"

Yu wasn't amused. "No, but don't worry, it will look good."

Ink turned on his tattoo needle. A small buzz radiated from it.

"Well, at least there's that," responded Jack.

Ink started to tattoo Jack's back. No words were spoken for a few minutes as Ink did his work and branded Jack. Ink looked up at Yu with his old eyes. Yu gave a sigh and left through the door they came in.

"Who's the cop?" Ink asked with a soft, grizzly voice.

Jack told Ink everything, leaving nothing out as well as explaining how he kidnapped the mole, leaving no connection to the Red Dragon or Fu. Ink didn't interrupt Jack once but continued his work on Jack's back. When Jack had finished his story, he waited silently for Ink to comment on it. Ink took a towel from his bag and wiped away some of the blood from Jack's back.

"You will be the only person in the Red Dragon to talk to the cop," said Ink. "The only Red Dragon member he should know about is you. Yu will supply you with cash for the cop when you need it."

"Understood. What does Lóng want me to do next?" Jack felt some blood dripping down his side. The pain not nearly as bad as he thought it would be; it was slowly becoming unnoticeable.

"Just lay there and look pretty," said a female voice from the railing. Jack, a little startled, looked toward the sound. Ink slapped Jack on the back of the head for moving. The woman of the voice slowly walked into Jack's view. She was young with an hourglass figure, wearing jean shorts and a tank top covered by a thin cardigan.

"Lei Lei, we're busy. Why are you here?" Ink growled.

"I was about to go shopping, but I heard there was something here I may like." She walked to the side of the pool table, the opposite of Ink, and eyed Jack's body. "You look better up close."

"So do you," replied Jack.

Lei Lei gave a small smile. "So, you noticed me the last time you were here?"

"How could I not," Jack said turning his head to the side to look at her. Ink slapped his head again.

Lei Lei bit her lower lip and laughed under her breath.

"Lei Lei, I want to do my work in peace," said Ink.

Lei Lei rolled her eyes. "Fine. I'll come back after lunch to get to know you a little better Jack." Lei Lei walked past Jack, ran her fingers through his hair.

Once her footsteps faded away, Ink continued to answer Jack's question. "Lóng was impressed by your ability to get a cop on our side so quickly and safely. He wants to use your gift to get back some of our rogue Red Poles."

"I assume I won't be going alone."

"That is correct. Yu and Li will accompany you. Yu will fill you in on the names and numbers."

"What if they want a bribe?"

"Try to avoid that," said Ink. "We don't have the money they will be asking for."

"Well, I hope you have enough money for me."

Ink didn't laugh at Jack's joke. "You will get paid in more ways than one."

Chapter 15

Sleeping Beauty

"Damn! You Americans can sleep through anything," Lei Lei commented loudly, waking Jack up from his nap on the pool table.

Jack laughed, but it turned into a wheeze of pain as he sat up from laying on his chest for hours.

"Need me to rub some lotion on it?" Lei Lei said as she placed a plastic bag with a yellow smiley face on the table.

Jack laughed the question away. "Thanks for the food. How long have I been asleep?" Jack opened the plastic bag and took out the white Styrofoam box.

"I don't know," Lei Lei said, "probably a couple of minutes because I ran into Ink on the way up here, which is why I came." She leaned on the pool table as Jack ate. "I was hoping to catch you alone to ask you some of my own questions." She leaned closer to Jack, and he noticed her sharp green eyes. "How does a sexy man like you end up in such a dirty business like this and so far away from home?"

"I pissed the wrong people off."

She raised an eyebrow, her face still coming closer. Jack wanted to back away, but the thoughts of upsetting the sister of the Dragon Head didn't go well in his mind. "My, they must have been pretty mad to make a big man like you run." Her voice slowed, and his heart raced.

"Well, they weren't that mad." Jack's stomach growled.

Lei Lei smiled. "We will continue that conversation later. You go ahead and eat." She stood back up.

Relief washed over Jack. "Thanks, I am a bit hungry." Lei Lei sat at a table and watched Jack eat. "So, how does it look?"

"Pretty good," commented Li as he entered the lounge. "Ink still has it."

"It never left him, like you," commented Lei Lei.

Li flipped her off. "Can we get going on with our business?" said Li, obviously wanting to move the conversation forward.

"What business?" asked Jack taking another bit of his Orange Chicken.

"Red Pole business. Did Lóng tell you not to be an ass?" Lei Lei asked Li.

"Yes mother," said Li. "He told me all the details too, so you don't have to worry."

"Can I at least finish my food?" Jack said, a tad bit bothered.

"We will have food at the meeting," snapped Li.

"Can I at least see what my new tattoo looks like?" Jack got up from the pool table.

"Turn around," Lei Lei ordered as she whipped out her phone and took a picture of Jack's tattoo. Jack put his shirt back on, then looked at the picture. He was impressed by the speed and detail that Ink did it in, though it had taken the majority of the day. No one would have known that though by just looking at it. The dragon's wingless body slithered up Jack's spine towards his head. Its red scales resembled the color of blood eerily well.

"Ready now?" Li stood next to the back exit.

Jack gave Lei Lei her phone back. "Yeah."

"Don't be a stranger," said Lei Lei as Li and Jack walked out.

"Don't worry, I won't," Jack replied with a wink. Li made a gagging sound, which Lei Lei shrugged off as she helped herself to Jack's Orange Chicken.

As Jack and Li walked down the back stairs, Li commented, "I've never seen her come on that hard to someone before."

"Well, foreigners are naturally hotter than natives." Jack slyly replied.

Li stopped at the bottom of the stairs as he rolled that thought over. "You're right." Li continued walking again. "Oh, also here's your pay for finding that rat." Li reached into his pocket and pulled out a dirty envelope filled with cash. Jack placed it in his pocket without counting the contents. He was just happy he had some money.

They got into a small, rusty PT Cruiser. While Li drove them to their destination, he filled Jack in on the plan. Jack listened, looking out the window at Hong Kong's countless bright signs.

"We are going to meet Boqin and get his sorry ass back home."

"Who's he?" asked Jack.

"An old wimp from back in the day that thinks he can be a Red Pole outside of the Red Dragon." Li giggled to himself. "Oh Boqin! Don't worry about the talking part, Jack. You just stand there looking intimidating, and he will fold up easily. Once the others see that, they will, too."

"Why? Do they have respect for him striking out on his own?" Jack's voice betrayed a bit of concern, but Li didn't hear it.

“I guess. But he’s not strong enough to stay there. Trust me. I know him.”

Jack didn’t reply to that and hoped Boqin hadn’t changed over the years, for both their sakes.

Chapter 16

Boqin

Boqin's platinum white hair stood out in the bright restaurant. Two men sat beside him. Their bodies were larger than Boqin's thin one. Four similarly dressed men, each with a blazer over a white t-shirt, were positioned at the corners of the partially filled restaurant. Boqin stood up, revealing his short stature, as he saw Li and Jack enter the establishment.

"Li! I still can't believe you're back! When did you arrive in Hong Kong?"

"A little more than a week ago."

Boqin shook Li's hand with both his own before offering a seat across from him. Jack stood behind Li, observing the surroundings discreetly. Li continued, "but what about you little Bo? A big Red Pole, I hear?" Mockery dripped from every word.

Boqin chuckled it off. The men sitting at his side showed no sign of amusement. Jack made a second glance at the other guards and noticed small bulges in their clothes. Jack knew they bulged because of handguns.

"Technically I'm not a Red Pole since I have two Red Poles under me," replied Boqin, his face happy but stern.

Li leaned back in his chair and gave a long whistle. "That's just…wow! Congrats man, anyone I know?"

"Probably not, just a couple of talented 49ers Lóng shafted." Boqin's tone sharpened.

Li didn't notice. "Well, I'm glad someone saw their talent. Speaking of Lóng, have you talked to him lately?"

"I haven't seen him since I left three…four years ago."

Li leaned forward on the table. "Well, I recently talked to him, and he told me he's in sort of a tight bind."

Boqin's smile faded; his eyebrows frowned. Li still didn't seem to notice. Jack wondered when Li would start becoming intimidating. Li continued, "He recently got a new supplier who has a lot more items to move than he anticipated and needs some extra hands and muscle. When he talked to me about it, the first person that came to my mind was you…"

"Where are they coming in?" Boqin interjected.

"The regular port like old times." A wide grin came across Li's face.

Boqin gave a single, soft laugh. "Old times? The old times when you pushed me off the pier during that one winter?"

"That was during the summer." Li's grin shrunk.

"Or the time you hid a snake in my bed?"

"It was a harmless garden snake."

"Or that time you left me in the bay a mile out from shore?"

"You still got back."

"You slept with my girlfriend!" Boqin's voice raised slightly, causing a few customers to look at his table.

"You weren't even dating." Li's grin was almost gone.

"She was still mine!" Boqin noticed the customers and took a second to calm himself. "Li, my entire life you have pushed me around. Taken what was mine. Given me shit all for a good laugh and like the wimp I was I took it, all of it, because you were the Dragon Head's 'son'." The two guards in the corner of the restaurant made their way towards them. "But times have changed. You left, he died, and an idiot inherited the Dragon Head. An idiot who couldn't even keep a rat out of it and if it wasn't for your dead mother, your brother would have been dead too, and you too if Spanish hitmen could do their jobs properly. Face it, your triad's time is over. Hong Kong is mine." The two guards beside him stood.

Li stood up. His face grew red, and for the first time he didn't have a response.

"Is the chatty Li speechless?" Boqin asked sarcastically as he picked up his spoon. "I'll keep that in mind when I want to shut you up next time." Boqin took a sip of his soup as the guards took a firm hold of Jack and Li's arms. "Mention one of your dead moms."

Boqin shooed them away with his empty spoon. They were escorted through the kitchen, completely ignored by the cooks and waiters even though Li was cursing at the top of his lungs. Two other guards stood at the back door, looking at their phones until they came up. They opened the door and Jack and Li were tossed out into the back alley.

Jack barely kept his feet under him as he ran into the wall. Li fell to his knees still cursing. "And another thing you sons of bitches! All of you! Let that mother…"

Li cursing was cut off. Jack turned around to see why as three of the four guards starting to slash Li on the ground with meat cleavers. The fourth came after Jack. He dodged his head as the guard's knife came down at it. He missed the head but found Jack's arm, skinning off a small piece of Jack's bicep. With his bleeding arm, Jack grabbed the hand that held the cleaver and pulled it close to his body for control. With his other hand, Jack tried to slam the back of the guard's head against the concrete wall. But the guard used his free hand to brace himself for the impact, then shifted his feet and swung his body around. Jack held the guard's right arm close to his chest, hitting his head against the wall. Jack caught a quick glimpse of Li on his back frantically kicking, punching, and cussing at the top of his lungs as the three guards slashed at any part they could. The guard fighting Jack took a step-in front of Jack to face him. Jack beat him to it by stepping in front of his foot, causing the guard to be off balance for a split second, which was enough for Jack. Using his hip and the arm, Jack threw the guard over his leg and toward the ground. Jack slipped his knee up against the guard's arm and quickly broke it at the elbow. The scream of pain and the sight of their triad brother caused the other guards to stop their assault as Jack held the cleaver at the man's neck, standing over him.

"We get the message!" Jack said sternly.

Jack shoved the guard toward them, pulled Li close to him and helped him up. Li continued to curse under his breath as they quickly walked away from the guards who stood motionless, watching them every step of the way, paying no attention to the other guard writhing in pain. Jack stared back, keeping the cleaver at the ready in case they thought the message had been lost on Jack and Li. Once the guards started helping their injured partner, Jack focused his attention back on Li. He was near the exit of the alleyway leaning on one of the buildings, the blood from his wounds creating a pool where he stood.

"Stay here, I'm getting the car." Jack took the keys from Li and ran to the car as Li breathed painfully. He tried to slow the bleeding of the larger wounds with his hands, but it still leaked through his fingers. Jack ran out of the alley and onto the sidewalk. The few people out and about gave him a second glance as they saw a tall American with blood on his arm and hands running through the crowds. Turning the corner, he saw the car surrounded by a few of Boqin's thugs. They leaned on it and laughed at something Jack didn't hear. Reaching the car, he yanked the man against the driver door off and got in. The thug's smiles turned to anger then mockery as Jack drove around the corner. Li was seated on the ground, his face paler than when Jack left him. Parking and getting out, Jack was able to get a good full look at Li's condition as he approached him. Cuts littered his arms. Some had pieces of flesh dangling off, showing some muscle and a little bone. Li's pants were stained with blood as it seeped through the fabric onto the alleyway. Jack threw one of Li's arms over his shoulder and carried him to the car. A few passing civilians stopped and observed Jack placing Li in the car. As he circled the car to the driver's seat Jack saw a young man on his cell phone, he assumed with the police. Jack sped off before anyone attempted to offer their help.

"How are you doing?" Jack asked Li as he dodged through the traffic.

"I've been better," responded Li in a weak voice, trying to wipe his tears with a shaking hand.

Jack gave out a chuckle, though his face didn't break a smile. "I bet. Don't worry, we will get you patched up real quick."

"I guess he was right," Li commented as Jack made a quick turn onto a one-way street.

"Right about what?" asked Jack. He wanted to keep Li talking to know Li was still breathing as his crying quietened.

"I'll bleed out like she did."

"Who?" Jack looked over as he wasn't following Li.

"My... My mom."

"How?" Jack asked. "Tell me the story, I need you to keep talking Li, I need you to stay with me."

"Before my dad kicked me out, he told me…He told me about the day of my birth…In a whore house…" Jack took another turn, missing a couple crossing the street by an inch. "She told him I was his son…Hoping he would help…" Li breathed out a single laugh as Jack dodged through the traffic, checking out his side mirrors as he heard faint sirens. "She forgot who he was…" Li's voice quivered as Jack crossed four lanes of traffic to turn to the correct street. "He left the room and barricaded the door shut…" The car jumped as they hit the curb of the sidewalk. "If it wasn't for my step-mom showing up with her personal doctor that followed her when she was pregnant…Both of us would have been dead. Sorry, Mom." Li closed his eyes as Jack pulled into the gym parking lot.

Jack carried Li up the flight of broken metal stairs, yelling as he approached the door.

"Open up Yu! Li got slashed!" Jack kicked the door when he reached it.

As soon as Yu opened the door, his face went white. "Shit man! Get in!" Yu demanded. He yelled at the pair of guys he was playing dominos with to get bandages. Yu frantically pushed the dominos and ashtrays off the pool table. Jack laid Li on the table as Yu rushed to a cabinet above a small sink and brought out a bottle of whiskey.

"How are you doing?" Jack inquired again.

"Didn't you already ask that?" asked Li.

Yu gave him a sip of the whiskey with Jack lifting his head. Li gave a loud cough, almost throwing it up. The two men returned from downstairs, carrying bandages and what also looked like a torn bedsheet. Jack didn't complain as he took some of the bandages. All the men wrapped up a limb, and Li cussed and yelled through his teeth through it all.

After fifteen minutes and another run for more bandages, Li was patched up. Yu gave him some painkillers. Yu and Jack moved him to the tattered couch as the other two guys went to take care of the car and get a hold of Ink. Jack and Yu sat beside each other on the blood covered table observing Li. He partially resembled a mummy in a museum.

"Who did this?" Yu asked solemnly.

"Boqin."

"What? Little Bo?" Disbelief was in Yu's voice.

"Little Bo isn't little anymore," said Jack. "He has two Red Poles and half the ports. The situation is worse than Lóng thought. How many Red Poles do we have?"

"Three." Yu gulped.

Jack kept his eyes on Li. "We need to keep our men off Boqin's turf because we can't deal with a triad war right now."

"But what about him?" Yu asked, his voice firm as he nodded at Li. "Are we just going to let them walk over us like that? Back when I was a 49er…"

"Back then you all had the muscle to back it up," Jack said bluntly, cutting Yu off. "From what I know, we don't have that same kind of power now. We are on the same playing field as everyone else. We are going to have to work for our meals or be a meal."

Chapter 17

Changing Wind

Inspector Ko observed the bleached concrete next to the industrial garbage can. He looked down the alley to see it was all washed recently. Inspector Chiu stood with the officers near the yellow crime tape that cut off the alley from the rest of the street. He had his pad and pen out, asking some of the bystander's short questions and jotting the answers. Once Chiu had finished with his last witness, he approached Ko, who was still standing near the trashcan, looking down the alley. Chiu tapped Ko on the shoulder and handed him his pad. Ko looked over all the answers briefly to get the basic idea of what possibly happened. Sounds of a fight had come down from the alley. A tall white man with a big beard had come running out and around the corner, brought a black, unlicensed PT Cruiser back, and helped his companion, who was suffering from several deep cuts and slashes, into the car and drove south. Ko gave the pad back to Chiu.

"Thoughts?" asked Chiu.

"Possibly an attempted robbery that went south but the store didn't call the police. And where's the bag of cash?" replied Ko.

"Triad?"

"More likely, it would fit their style. I mean, we've seen some small stuff supposedly connected to the triad." Ko looked back to the bleached spot. "But why the blood now?"

"American?" asked Chiu.

"Too much of a coincidence. It wouldn't hurt to ask him some questions, though. This could help lift the blinders off of Su - pardon, Chief Executive Su - and his high horse."

Chiu smiled, as his partner seemed more like himself than he had in a long time. Ko's phone rang. He paid no attention to it since Chiu had it and was already answering it. Ko didn't listen to Chiu's one-word questions and answers. Ko was contemplating who the white companion was. He stood up and turned to Chiu, who had just hung up. His face was soft, a rare thing since people called him the 'silent statue' sometimes.

"Who was it?" Ko asked.

"Fu."

"What does he want?" Ko requested in the nicest tone, the tone he used to refer to Fu ever since he started working for him.

"The mole's gone," said Chiu calmly.

Ko's eyes widened as he huffed air through his nose. He glared at Chiu, who kept his eyes toward the floor. Ko turned around and started kicking the garbage can till most of the trash flew out of it and the middle of it was completely crushed in on itself. The cops in the street jumped but resisted their instincts to look. Bystanders stopped and stared at Ko. Once he was done, he bowed his head and walked close enough to Chiu that only he could hear him.

"How the hell did they find him? What happened to his security?"

"No security," answered Chiu sadly. The crowd had started to move again.

"No security?" Ko's voice grew to a harsh whisper. "Just because they haven't tried anything in a few years means he's safe forever? That the triad will just forget what he did? Did they at least have him report where he was going or who he was seeing?"

"No." Chiu's tone was confident now, more professional.

"I knew I should have pressed him harder to let me do his security! Of course, he didn't want family to do it!" sneered Ko through his teeth. He looked to the sky. It was a bright blue, not a cloud in sight. Tears formed in his eyes. "This is my fault," said Ko. "Phone please."

Chiu handed Ko his phone. He took it and walked away from Chiu. Ko tapped the phone and placed it to his ear. He took a few long breaths as it rang. Then she picked up.

"Hello? Mom? Listen. I need you to sit down."

Chapter 18

Fan and Sandal

Li felt dead, though he was quite alive. His arms and legs were stiff and beat like a drum. He opened his eyes to a ceiling fan slowly rotating, making a white noise he fell asleep often to. Turning his head, he looked out the window that had a similar view to his apartment. Li gently opened his hand and felt the fabric of the bed: silk, the same as his apartment. He concluded he was in his apartment.

"Good morning," said Jack, coming into Li's view with a glass of water and a bottle of pills.

Li tried to sit up, but found that wouldn't be possible since he couldn't bend his arms. "How long was I out?" he asked as Jack helped him reposition.

"Two days. Though you came in and out a lot. When you did, Ink would just shove more painkillers and antibiotics in you."

"That explains why I don't remember waking up," commented Li. Jack opened the bottle of pills, placed a tablet in Li's mouth, and helped him with the water. "Thanks," said Li.

"For everything, you're the first person that actually cares about me,"

"Your siblings care for you a lot," responded Jack.

"They will have a limit. You are the second person who doesn't seem to have one,"

"That's what friends are for," Jack said half honestly, with the feeling of guilt following.

Li smiled and chuckled. "Did you ever think you would end up being friends with the guy you were trying to kidnap?"

Jack rolled his eyes with a smile. "I was trying to get a job, man, but I didn't expect to be saving your ass this many times." They laughed. A small wave of grief washed up in Jack for not saving Jones and shame for not really trying.

"But honestly doc? How am I physically?" Li asked, his voice and tone seemed to be back to his old self.

"Not in the best shape. They had almost hacked a piece of your arm off, but Ink sewed you up well. You lost a lot of blood. Yu said we used up all the reserve of your blood type to keep you alive. Ink and Yu are resupplying that today."

Li nodded, looking around his bedroom. Dirty white walls surrounded him with cheap modern art and a flatscreen facing him beside the door that led to the rest of his apartment. "How long till I can fend for myself?" Li asked.

"A week of taking it super easy, then maybe you can do some things. A couple of places where you have a deep gash will take a long time." Li nodded, observing his mummy arms. Red splotches showed through. As if reading Li's mind, Jack said, "Ink should be arriving soon."

"So, what's the plan?"

"I'm going to move in to help you at night and…"

"No, what's the plan? What are we going to do about Boqin?" Li's eyes dropped to Jack's bandage. His blood was not showing up nearly as much as Li's, but it was still there.

"We aren't going to do anything," said Ink as he entered the bedroom. "Jack, Li and I need a moment."

"Of course." Jack stood up and left the room, closing the door behind him. He took a few steps away from the door before tiptoeing back to it to listen. Eavesdropping was Spy 101.

Ink sat down in the stained wood chair next to the window. He wore a black Changshan with gold accent at the wrist and collar. "You look less shitty today," said Ink.

Li made a face, as if Ink had told him he was the prettiest girl at prom. "You're too sweet, really."

Ink didn't laugh like normally. "Ready to listen?"

The light in Li's face faded away as he nodded. Ink then gave Li - and Jack on the other side of the door - the rundown. "Shan and Jinjiang were picked up by the Grey Mountain and Yellow Sun respectively."

"Those…"

Ink jerked his hand up and interrupted Li. "I said listen. They are out. Boqin is the strongest as we expected. That was why we advised you to let Lóng handle him. Tao isn't that far behind Boqin, we think. But we don't know where he is. Xing has a lot of 49ers and may be looking to expand. The rest are stable. Some guys think they heard Zemin talking about joining forces with Enlai. Gui is still in prison. Duyi, Heng, and Tung aren't expanding at all and Chi looks like he's struggling the most."

Li didn't say anything as he processed all this new information. He was learning he wasn't that big of a man anymore. "So, where does that leave us?" he finally asked.

"Upper end of the middle, with some open positions."

"What kind of open positions?" asked Li.

"The kind you don't want open long. That's why I'm here and telling you all this." Ink slowly stood up. "Lóng would like you to become the White Paper Fan for the Red Dragon."

"Holy shit!" responded Li. He shot upright in bed, followed by slowly laying back down. "The fan, huh? Well of course, I accept. I'm just a tad surprised as I thought that was Yu's job?"

"It was, but Lóng wants him to focus on being the Straw Sandal and getting those Red Poles back. Lóng wants Jack to go with him as a bodyguard. They should be paying Chi a visit tomorrow."

"Makes sense," said Li.

Jack stepped quietly away from the door; he could tell their conversation was about to end. He laid on the couch in the small living room and closed his eyes, pretending to be asleep.

He must have actually fallen asleep, because the room was dark when he woke up. Ink had already left; Li was still in his room, sleeping with the glass of water and bottles of drugs besides his bed. Jack rubbed his eyes and quietly left the apartment to process the new knowledge he had gained. He wanted to develop a strategy for his next step and see who he would run into that night.

Chapter 19

Morning Beers

"Calling it a night already?" Jack shouted out to Saul as Jack got out of a cab.

Saul broke out in a smile as he walked out of the Boom Club. "Yeah, we had too many bartenders tonight, so they sent me home." Saul placed his pay check in his wallet. "The better question is why are you here without anyone?"

Jack put his hands in his pockets. "Just woke up and I thought I would start the day off with a good drink and some good conversation."

Saul laughed. "Amy wasn't here tonight; she only comes like once a month."

Jack tilted his head like a confused puppy. "Okay."

"So, you're saying you wanted to get a beer to wake up to at…" Saul checked the time on his smartphone, "one in the morning?"

Jack kicked the ground. "Well, maybe I just wanted to talk to you and hear the rest of that story?" Jack was trying to defend himself like a schoolboy when his buddies find out about his crush on a girl.

Saul shook his head at him. "I don't doubt that, but that wasn't the main reason for you coming over at this hour. Listen, I'll go ahead and give you a hand." Saul took out a business card from his wallet and handed it to Jack. "Here's her business card, so you have a way of getting hold of her when you're ready instead of waiting to run into her. That can be a little creepy." Saul raised his hand as he saw a cab coming down the road. "But don't forget that I gave you a fair warning. If she turns you down like all the others, don't take it personally." The cab stopped, and Saul got in while Jack stared at the business card in thought.

"Do you do this with every new 49er?" asked Jack.

Saul signaled the cab driver to give him a second. "No, just the ones that feel the weight of the business they are in. Those are the people who need a friend on the outside the most. But treat her right, ok? That's another reason I'm giving you her number; I don't think you will hurt her or hold a grudge if she says no. Don't prove me wrong." Saul's voice was the same chipper tone as always, but his brown eyes were grave and dark.

"I promise, I won't."

Saul gave him a thumbs up and said goodbye. His cab drove off into the busy streets of Hong Kong. Jack stood there and watched the cab leave his view, thinking about what Saul said until he was interrupted by a familiar voice calling his name. He turned to see Lei Lei walking away from a group of women. She wore a tight black club dress that was questionably short. He put his hands back in his pockets, hiding the business card.

"Hey Lei Lei, what are you doing here?"

"Just clubbing with my girls," she said, tilting her head in the direction of the group she left walking down the street. "What are you doing here? Some unwinding?" She took a step closer, eyes welcoming. Her high heels almost made her the same height as him.

"Just thought I would come get a drink and see who I would run into." He kept his body still.

"Well, I hope I didn't disappoint." She took a step closer. Her dress almost touched his shirt.

"You didn't." Jack took small breaths.

Lei Lei took a deep inhale, pressing her chest against his, releasing it with a, "Well, how about we go back to my place for drinks?"

Jack released a nervous "Sure" and quietly followed her to a cab which took them to her apartment in the better part of Hong Kong. Through the drive, he reminded himself that this was a perfect moment to gain a great ally but also a moment to make a great enemy if he angered her.

When they reached her home Jack held the cab door open for Lei Lei. Glancing across the street, he thought he saw Mallory standing beside a homeless man. She was dressed like she was about to go on a date with him. Jack turned away and saw Lei Lei standing a step away with her hand stretched out. He grabbed her hand to escape his grief.

Chapter 20

Empty Wishes

"So, what are your secrets?" asked Lei Lei as she sat on her bed, after giving Jack a tour of her expensive apartment. Jack stood next to the window, gazing at Hong Kong shining brightly with all its new buildings slicing through the night sky.

"None really, just a typical mobster getting used to his new mob." He took another sip of his Scotch with ice. "Why do you ask?"

He turned around. Lei Lei propped herself up on one arm as the other held her Scotch, straight up. Her hair flowed down the left side of her head, concealing part of her face in a shadow and highlighting the red streaks in it.

"I like to know if the men I sleep with are single or not, though it typically doesn't change anything."

Jack looked down at his drink. "I'm single."

"How long?" Lei Lei asked quickly.

Jack forced a chuckle out of himself. "Just six months, but it was a terrible breakup." Jack rolled the ice cube around in his drink. Mallory wasn't fond of Scotch that much; she liked the fruity drinks.

"Who dropped who?" Lei Lei's voice had lost its seductive tone and sounded normal for the first time to Jack, almost sincere.

"I dumped her because I knew I was about to be on the run." The longer he stared at his round glass, the more it resembled the tunnel he traveled through. He sat beside Lei Lei on the bed made of memory foam. "We were engaged for a bit," Jack added before even thinking.

"Oh! I love proposal stories!" said Lei Lei, adjusting on the bed to face him. "How did you do it?"

Jack smiled as he told the story for the first time. "It was sort of spur of the moment. I was about to leave to do my first pickup across the border alone. Call it fear, but I didn't want to lose her while I was gone. So, I bought some stuff and got to her place before she got off work to make her a really fancy dinner with candles, a three-course meal, the works. However, thinking a lot about how it was going to look and what I was going to say, I had forgotten that her stove and oven didn't work well. A few minutes later smoke is coming out of the oven and the stove still wasn't on. That's when I heard the door unlock and the fire alarm go off. No lie, I jumped to the front door and shut it on her, told her to hang on just a minute while I grabbed a towel and started waving it like a madman in front of the fire alarm. It didn't work well. I took the alarm out and shoved it in the couch cushion. I turned around."

Thomas saw Mallory in his mind, clear and pristine, standing in her apartment door that night. White shoes. White slacks, too, tight and form-fitting. Red roses imprinted her loose, black silk blouse. Though his story included smoke, his memory held her beach perfume unaltered. He always wanted his home to smell like that. The home he wanted, the home he pined for, was that doorway she stood in.

Jack continued the story. "She was standing in the doorway, smoke rolling past her. She looked around at the disaster of a meal in the kitchen and the unlit candles on the table with the ring box on it. She's pretty smart and said 'yes' before I could even say anything." Jack wiped a tear away. "It's more funny than romantic but it was our story."

Lei Lei took a deep breath and said. "It isn't romantic, but it is sweet."

"I guess, but doesn't really matter anymore."

"It sounds like you need some help forgetting her?" Lei Lei ran her fingers through his hair.

Jack tensed up slightly. "I don't want to forget her. I just want to forget the pain."

Jack started to take another sip, but Lei Lei pulled the glass away from him and set it on the nightstand next to a picture of her in a wedding dress.

"Well, I can help you with that too." She reached behind him and scratched the back of his head as she gave him a long kiss. Jack wished he didn't enjoy it. He wished he didn't kiss her back. He wished the guilt didn't leave him as she placed him down on her bed. He wished Mallory was still alive but wishing didn't make any of it real.

Jack woke up. The light trickle of rain descending on Hong Kong distracted Jack from getting up. He looked beside him at Lei Lei, naked and fast asleep on her bed. Her hair sprawled over the bed like her body. Jack shook his head and slowly got up. He dressed himself and quietly left as Lei Lei snored. Riding the elevator, he tried to rationalize his actions to himself as he felt guilt and shame slowly encroach themselves on him, but it didn't shake the feeling of betraying Mallory. As he left the building, he attempted to place his mind on other problems that he needed to address: which Red Poles Yu would go after first, how he was going to find The Twelve by getting closer to Lóng through Lei Lei. But the feelings didn't leave him.

Exiting the building, Jack saw the rain begin to fall harder. He looked through the thin traffic for a taxi, but saw something more intriguing. Across the street, he saw the same homeless man from earlier sitting at a bus stop covering, staring straight at him again. A large scarf covered the man's face. Checking both ways, Jack walked over to the bus stop. The homeless man didn't leave when Jack sat down with him. Jack shook off the rain and glanced at the man. His shoes were old combat boots that had lost their color. His black cargo pants were stained, and his hoodie had holes in it. His face and hands were covered with a rough looking cloth. At a closer look, Jack saw the walking stick resembled more of a metal Jō staff than a walking stick.

"So," Jack said, looking at his hands as he wiped the rain off his pants. The man kept his eyes on Jack. "Have we met before?"

The homeless man said nothing.

"Was it at a party you crashed?"

The man slowly let his staff rotate towards Jack, laying to rest one end on Jack's head. He asked in a slurred, muffled voice, "Where's Lóng?"

Jack froze, moving only his mouth to answer. "I can find out for you."

The man lifted his Jō off Jack's head.

"But," said Jack, "it will take some time since he has a whole crew looking for you."

"Not a problem," said the man. "Why should I trust you?" He placed the Jō back on Jack's head.

"Because I didn't shoot you at first sight," Jack said, nonchalantly staring back at him.

"You have no gun. Why should I trust you?"

"You're not an average assassin, are you?" asked Jack leaking out only a hint of surprise. The Jō slid down Jack's face and stopped at his throat, pressing softly against his windpipe.

"No. Why should I trust you?"

Jack resisted swallowing, and with a quickly drying throat said, "Because I don't care if he dies."

"I don't want him dead, but speak of this, and you will be." With that, he took the Jō off Jack's neck and left without another word.

Jack looked the opposite direction of the assassin to see a police car turning onto the street they occupied. Jack quickly took out his phone and pretended to do something on it until they passed. He glanced over at the seat where the assassin sat to see he had left a small card. Jack examined it. It was a stockbroker business card. He turned it over to see only one word written on the other side.

Dumpster.

Chapter 21

Limited Forgiveness

Chi stood in front of an elderly man selling fish, and collected his protection money. The older man reluctantly thrust a small wad of cash into Chi's hand and mumbled under his breath curses toward Chi as he left, who was counting his money.

"Chi, how are you?" asked Yu as he and Jack approached him in the street market.

Chi stuffed the money in his pocket before acknowledging them. "Yu! I'm good, I'm good. Just collecting some dues."

"Thought that was a job for 49ers?" asked Jack curiously, though that was not the way Chi took it.

"They usually do," answered Chi bitterly, "but they have had some trouble with the old fisherman, so that's why I'm here. I take it you're the Lumberjack?"

Jack tilted his head, his eyes narrowed as if reading what Chi said to make more sense of it.

Chi chuckled. "Yeah, you're him. That's what everyone calls you because, you know, you look like one."

Jack remembered the bald-headed fighter who first called him that. "Well, I guess I am then. News travels that fast here."

"Also," said Chi, "Heard you and Li got cut up pretty bad." Eyeing Jack's bandage, he gave a louder laugh showing off his jagged teeth under his pencil mustache. "Guess it wasn't as bad as they said."

Jack clenched his jaw and smiled only for a second.

Yu intervened. "Yeah, well, Li's fine too. What other rumors are floating around that you've heard?"

Chi nodded, took out a pack of cigarettes, and said, "Heard that Lóng is trying to rebuild the Red Dragon after his failure of inheritance."

"Victim of circumstances," Yu quickly pointed out.

Chi shrugged his shoulders. "Sure, whatever helps him sleep at night."

Jack gave a genuine smile and said, "Did you know that the mole responsible for it went missing a couple of days ago?"

Chi's cheerful face dimmed slightly. Yu started to clench his jaw now.

Jack continued, "I guess Boqin's men forgot to tell you that."

"Happens in this kind of business," said Chi, a small tremor in his hand as he puffed on his cigarette. "Have to be strong and smart to survive, or be allied with the strong."

"Who are you allied with?" Jack asked, looking at Chi who did not look back. "Because this chance to come back is limited to this moment. Forgiveness is limited to this moment."

Jack looked away, and Chi's shoulder's relaxed. "One time?" Chi drew a long inhale from his cigarette and let it out with a quick sigh. "Rackets don't bring in as much as they use to."

"A gift will be offered to those who repent," said Yu.

Chi's head shook as he looked toward the road behind Jack and Yu.

"A gift that keeps on giving?" asked Jack.

Chi looked at Jack, who started to hum 'The Wheels on the Bus' nursery rhyme. A smile emerged in the corner of Chi's mouth, and he said, "I like the sound of that."

Chi and Jack shook hands. Yu gave Chi his information to work out the details later. After they had said their goodbyes, Jack and Yu left Chi to his business. Jack had a grin on his face but Yu didn't. Once they were out of earshot, Yu voiced his concerns.

"What the shit was that?" said Yu. "I don't remember Lóng making you the Straw Sandal! If you do that kind of shit again, I will personally cut you a thousand times!" Yu kept his voice low, but he spoke with a sharpness in his words.

"It got him back in the Red Dragon didn't it?" asked Jack in a calm, carefree voice.

"At the cost of a bus route?! I'm not sure if anyone told you, but we don't have any bus routes! All we got are a dozen restaurants, a few clubs, a couple of whore houses and a few drug dealers. That's it. No buses."

"But Enlai does."

"So? We don't have the force to take it from him, and I thought we were supposed to be keeping ourselves out of a triad war?"

"I wasn't thinking about using force. Well, not our force at least."

Chapter 22

Heavy Badge

Fu sat in his older black car with tinted windows and watched the bus stop on the opposite side of the street. He looked down at the envelope he received the day before filled with new, irresistible hundred-dollar bills and a bus time bulletin with several different times and bus stop locations highlighted. Fu checked the time on his car's analog clock. Five minutes till the bus arrived. Fu perused the bus stop again. Two men sat on the bench smoking cigarettes, sloppy in their dress when compared to Fu's attire. He wore a Polo shirt tucked into his blue jeans; the two young men wore dirty shorts and t-shirts that looked like they hadn't seen a washer for a while. Fu placed the envelope in his glove compartment and pulled out the black handgun he had been issued when he became a cop. He pulled out his badge and held it in his right hand and the gun in his left. The badge seemed heavier than usual.

Fu looked back up to see the bus pulling up to the stop ahead of schedule. The two young men got up and waited for a few passengers to get off before entering the bus themselves. Fu's heart sped up as he hid his gun and badge before getting out of the car. He quickly crossed the street. Through the bus's front window, Fu could see the two men talking to the driver. As he grew closer, Fu saw the driver reach down and pull up a wad of cash. One of the young men took it as the other blocked the view of the passengers. But Fu could see quite well. He pulled out his badge and tapped it against the front window, catching their attention. Fu thought it would be simple: they would walk out and try to lie their way out of it, maybe even bribe him. He wouldn't give in, he would cuff them, and that would be that.

It wasn't like that at all. As soon as they caught a glimpse of the badge, they bolted. The man with the cash grabbed the driver, pulled out a knife and held the driver hostage. At the same moment, Fu dropped his badge and pulled out his gun, aiming it at the blade holder. The other young man hid behind his friend, peeping his head out to see what was happening. Fu didn't have the cleanest of shots on the thug.

"Drop the knife and step out of the bus!" Fu demanded. "This is your only warning."

"You drop it!" responded the thug, pushing his head forward with his chin up. His prideful motion gave Fu a much cleaner shot, which he instinctively took. Blood splattered onto the bus's ceiling. The driver dropped to the floor and curled up into a ball as the thug fell backward, landing on his companion. Fu dashed into the bus, his gun at the ready, and found the other thug sitting on the floor with blood-splattered hands above his head. The thug's partner lay beside him, dead.

Cops arrived. Some reporters too. Fu went back to the office. Filled out paperwork. Clocked out. Went grocery shopping and went home. He wondered why he was acting like it was another day at the office.

Fu's apartment door slowly closed behind him, as did the day. He held a plastic bag of groceries and his wife's prescription. His hands still shook from the bus shooting earlier. The bonus from Jack was helping the bills but not Fu's nerves at the moment. He walked through the unorganized living room and into the kitchen on the left. A pot of cooked noodles sat beside a sink with a couple of open bottles of spices and a baking sheet of cooked salmon.

The sound of gagging erupted from the bathroom. Fu dropped everything and dashed to the bathroom across the living room, with his hand on his gun. He stopped and peeked through the half-opened door to his wife's feet as she kneeled over the toilet. The sound of vomiting followed another short gag. Fu took his gun and placed it in the drawer beside the bathroom before going to his wife's aid.

She still had her pajamas on and was holding half her hair back with one hand as the other was on the toilet seat. She glanced back at her husband as he knelt beside her and took the job of holding back her hair.

"I'm sorry," she whispered with sweat and tears on her face before facing the toilet again and vomiting. Chewed-up noodles and salmon spilled into the toilet water.

"I'm sorry," she started again. "I thought since I craved it, it would taste good or something, I'm sorry, sorry."

Fu calmly shushed her as he rubbed her arm.

"I hate those pills," she finally cried out with empty lungs, resting her head on the toilet seat.

"Me too," Fu calmly said holding back his tears as he thought of the cash in his pocket and that one doctor. "Me too."

Chapter 23

Bad Lies

The pawn shop sat between an old restaurant and a shady loan business. Iron bars covered all the windows, making the welcome sign seem not that welcoming. Jack told the cab driver to wait for him as he entered the pawn shop. The driver yelled at him that it would cost extra. Jack ignored it, his mind set on his first collection.

The smell of curry hit Jack like a slap. It funneled to him through the tight corridor of shelves filled with paperback books, tiny statues, kitchenware, and more junk than Jack had ever seen. A man in his forties sat behind a glass case filled with cheap jewelry. His back was hunched and he was reading a western romance novel. Jack walked up and tapped on the glass counter.

"What you buying?" the owner asked, annoyed, without even looking up. Jack tapped the glass again. The owner rolled his head up to look at Jack. His annoyed face was washed away by fear.

"You the new collector?" The owner's voice was quivering as he asked.

Jack nodded. The owner closed his book and opened a drawer behind him with a key. He turned around with a wad of cash and gave it to Jack. Jack flipped through it once, noticing immediately it wasn't enough.

"I'm not new to this," Jack said, sounding bored but still a little nervous. "So, you need to pay me the right amount and extra for my inconvenience."

The owner frowned and opened his mouth to protest, but Jack cut him off. "You can either pay the hospital or me. Your choice."

The owner closed his mouth and gave Jack the rest of the money. Jack said nothing else and left.

As Jack was telling the driver where to take him, his phone rang and he answered.

"So, I hear you have been making some big waves recently?" said Lei Lei over the phone.

Jack chuckled. "Hey, just trying to do my job." He sat in a cab, observing the business card the assassin gave him.

"But really, taking over the talks with Chi, promising stuff you don't have, then using the cop you just got on the payroll to get said stuff? I'm a little turned on. Though, Yu is pissed at you."

Jack looked around for the business. "Yeah, I'm not surprised by that. I am surprised how you know about the cop." Jack faked concerned in his voice.

Lei Lei giggled. "Lóng told me. You honestly don't think I just shop all day and have affairs all night, do you?"

Jack forced an awkward chuckle as it clicked she was married. "I guess I underestimated you. I assumed he kept you out of the loop for safety."

"Safety?" Her voice sounded offended. "If my brother didn't pick up the mantle dad had left I would have been a big contender for picking it up. Though honestly," her voice grew soft again, "I'm glad he took the job. I enjoy being the Deputy. It's like a hobby that pays, better than actually working."

Jack stopped staring into the passing streets as he fit pieces of the puzzle together in his head. "Yeah, and I wouldn't have been able to have such a fun time with you if you were the Dragon Head. Speaking of, how is he?"

"He's still on edge since the attempt on his life. He's been prepping up a new safe house and just the regular Dragon Head duties."

"I take it no leads on the assassin?"

"No, but I gave Lóng some ideas on how to deal with him when we find him." Lei Lei chuckled maliciously.

Jack's cab came to a stop in front of a massive skyscraper. "I bet. Hey, I got to go, but I will call you later, alright?" Jack paid the cab driver and left the car.

"Sure, what are you doing?"

Jack looked over the crowd of people hustling from one building to another. "Apartment searching, don't want to live with Li forever. He's making great progress, and I don't want to be there when he starts going out and bringing girls home."

Lei Lei laughed. "I'm glad you're thinking ahead. What kind of apartment are you thinking of?"

Jack approached the alleyway to his right. "Some place simple and roomy."

"Ok, well keep me informed on how it goes. I'm not going to let you get something hideous. I refuse to sleep in an ugly apartment and if I do, I'll just leave before you wake up."

Jack laughed as he looked down the alley to see a dumpster. "Don't worry, I won't. And I promise I won't do that again. I'm about to walk into the apartment now, so I have to go. I'll talk to you later."

Jack hung up after Lei Lei said goodbye, and walked toward the dumpster. He kept his distance as he checked around the dumpster for any sign of the homeless assassin. There wasn't even a sign of anyone living there. Jack looked at the time when he heard a soft voice say, "Smoke." Jack casually took out a cigar and reluctantly lit it.

"Don't speak unless your mouth is covered."

Jack took a puff, using his palm to hide his mouth as the gruff voice had commanded.

"What do you want Lóng for?" Jack asked.

"Why don't you care for Lóng?" the voice asked back.

"I don't care who pays me."

"Lie. You would have reported me, but you didn't. Why?"

Jack leant against the rough wall, torn between being impressed at this man's abilities or questioning his ability to lie. He thought for a second in silence, considering what this man wanted. Then the thought hit him as if the wall he leaned on toppled on him. Jack took another puff. "Because, maybe we want him for the same thing?"

"I don't want money," he hissed at Jack.

"I don't either, like you said I would have reported you by now. Why do you want him?"

A silence followed Jack's question. Jack had a growing sense that this man didn't just know The Twelve like Golay in Amsterdam did. Jack suspected this man had worked for them.

"Where?" the man said, finally breaking the silence.

"My place, you should be able to find it. Come at your convenience."

Jack dropped the cigar and left without a word.

Chapter 24

Floating Meeting

Enlai walked with vigor toward the boathouse Boqin owned. The boat sat in the middle of an empty harbor, empty because on this sunny day most of the other boats were out enjoying the weather. Enlai was followed by two of his 49ers, both armed, just like he would when he was under the Red Dragon. Enlai wore a sports coat that made his companions look underdressed. He usually wore a 'wife beater' but knew if he wanted to get what he wanted he would need to dress to impress. Two large men in plain black suits and no ties stepped out from below the ship and onto the deck. Their uniforms were a little worn - some seams coming undone on their sleeves - but they still looked more mature than Enlai's own guards. He knew it would be like pulling teeth to get his men to dress like that. The two suited guards blocked the way onto the boat as Enlai approached.

"He only wants you to board, unarmed," said one of the guards.

Enlai gave a huff of disagreement as he took out his handgun and handed it to his men. The two suited guards parted and allowed Enlai on the boat, alone. The houseboat seemed old-fashioned from the outside, something cheap from the seventies. But when Enlai went down below, he was astonished at what he found: a full bar greeted him with large glass shelves housing vast assortments of local and foreign alcoholic beverages. The bar curved to his right to an open space with light brown armchairs and small tables for drinks. All the chairs faced the same general direction, away from Enlai and towards a large 4K TV. Boqin sat in the middle of the area, watching the World Cup and nursing a Scotch. Enlai's frustration settled down, and he approached Boqin slowly as he saw that the rumors were true.

"Enlai, happy to see you. Grab a drink and have a seat," said Boqin, looking over his shoulder.

Coming around the corner, Enlai saw a bartender with a small soul patch on his chin tending to the bar. Enlai ordered a German beer and had a seat beside Boqin, who had returned his attention to the match.

"I take it you heard about my bus route?" asked Enlai.

"Heard the cops got a hold of it. Bad timing can be a bitch," responded Boqin, still watching the game between Spain and Brazil, two football giants who held nothing back.

"I don't think it was due to bad timing," Enlai suggested, looking at his beer.

"Why do you say that?"

The referee pulled a yellow card on a Brazilian player who slid into his opponent's leg, dislocating the knee.

"Because the cop was off duty but had his badge and gun on him."

Boqin kept his eyes on the TV and asked, "So? Most cops have a gun on them at all times, he must have just gotten off work."

The Spanish team was in the face of the referee as their teammate was placed on a stretcher.

Enlai tightened his grip on his beer. "Then why are Chi's men hanging out at the bus stops?"

Boqin stopped himself from taking a sip of his Scotch.

The Spanish team slowly dispersed from the referee, still unhappy.

"Chi?" remarked Boqin. "Chi doesn't have the balls to tip off the cops. And if he did, then just take it back. He's nothing compared to you."

"I would, but I don't think he did. I think the Red Dragon did. And I believe he's on their payroll now."

The match started again with a free kick. Four Brazilians lined up to form a wall to protect the goal.

"The Red Dragon? What makes you think that?" Boqin looked at Enlai, granting him his full attention.

"Because he has some new 49ers and they were blue lanterns in the Red Dragon." Enlai took a sip of his beer to calm his growing frustration.

"So," said Boqin, "either he convinced them to switch, which is unlikely, the Red Dragon gave him some men and he went and took it himself, or they took it and used it as a bartering chip."

The Spaniard kicked the ball into the face of one of the Brazilian players's face, knocking him unconscious.

Boqin turned it off before the Brazilians reacted. "Either way, what are you going to do about it?" asked Boqin. He sat his Scotch down and shifted in his seat to face Enlai better.

Enlai did the same and gave his answer. "That's why I'm here. If it were just Chi alone, I would end him and take back what is mine. But it isn't just him, and though the Red Dragon has lost a few Red Poles, they are still possibly one of the strongest forces in Hong Kong."

"No." Boqin's voice was stern and grave. His eyes narrow and body tense. "The Red Dragon is still a force to be cautious of, but Lóng isn't half the man his father was. They will gain support naturally due to their heritage, but time will corrode it away. What doesn't corrode, I will cut off."

A chill went up Enlai's spine. Boqin smiled and pulled out a small gold box from his pocket and continued. "But that is for a later matter. What you want is your bus route back."

Enlai didn't speak. Boqin opened the box and took out two tiny paper pouches and placed them on the table between them. "Because of the situation, though," said Boqin, "it would be unwise to try and take it back now, even with my help at the moment."

Boqin slid a bag toward Enlai as he poured the white powdery contents onto the polished end table and said, "But, in time, I can see us taking more than just a bus route."

Boqin pulled a hundred-dollar bill out and rolled it into a small straw, which he used to sniff up the line of cocaine. He took a gasp, then said, "In time, all of Hong Kong can be ours." Boqin extended the rolled-up bill to Enlai. "Want a hit?"

Chapter 25

New Home

"Ta-da," said Lei Lei, pulling her hands away from Jack's eyes to reveal his new apartment with a wall-sized window looking out onto Hong Kong's business district from thirty stories up. The open loft apartment had only two columns, a door on the left to the bedroom and a short hallway out of sight that led to the bathroom.

"Damn Lei Lei! You outdid yourself. How much is it?" Jack walked around the apartment, observing the brick walls and wood floor.

"It's free," she responded, with a hint of pride.

Jack stopped and stared at her with a raised eyebrow. "Nothing's free, least of all this. What does it cost?"

She chuckled. "True, I guess you could say the cost is hospitality." She walked over to him in her black leggings and a gray cardigan over a black tank top.

"Hospitality of what?" Jack asked, concerned with who he was going to share his space with.

"Lóng wants this to be an outpost in case we get into a 'war', as he put it." She walked past him and up to the window.

"Is that why he's been gone?" Jack asked accusingly, looking over his shoulder at her.

Lei Lei's tone didn't change from its monotone type as she responded. "With the attack on Li and the attempt on his life, he thinks the renegade Red Poles may become more aggressive. So, he wants to prepare for the worst. Hence this and his business trip."

Jack was tempted, but didn't pursue to snoop about the trip. He walked up beside her and rubbed his shoulder against hers. "And all this time I thought it was because I slept with you."

She laughed. "If that were the case, I would be housing half of Hong Kong."

They both giggled as they stared out the window at Hong Kong. Its streets were full with tiny specks of people as they walked past the towering buildings. A silence started to grow between them, but was cast away quickly with Lei Lei saying, "You're going to need a good interior decorator to at least make this bearable."

Jack smiled. "Don't worry about that, I know one."

"Who?" Lei Lei's voice was genuinely curious for the first time.

"Meldon Architect Firm has some interior designers. I met one of them at The Boom."

"What's their name?" Seriousness was in her voice.

Jack considered lying, but that hadn't been doing too well for him recently. "Amy something, why?"

"Amy Smith?" Lei Lei's eyes widened as her face brightened up, her mouth curling a smile.

"I take it you know her?" assumed Jack, not sure if that was good yet or not.

"Of course! She would be perfect to decorate this place; her style is amazing."

Jack smiled back. "She does seem to have an artistic view." He looked around the room wondering what Amy would do with it.

"Yeah, she's great too, one of the sweetest people I know."

"I know," added Jack, without thinking.

"Really?" Lei Lei followed.

Jack realized that his comment was too sincere, too infatuated, too honest. He turned around to see Lei Lei with her hands on her hips and her head leaning to one side, waiting for an answer.

"Really what?" Jack asked, leaning his head forward as if he didn't hear her. He hoped playing dumb would help too.

"Is this the girl you've been talking to at The Boom?"

Jack tried to ask another question for time to think, but Lei Lei didn't pay attention to him.

"Holy shit it is!"

Jack prepared for the worst.

"Holy shit you two would be perfect together."

Jack crinkled his face at the surprising answer. She didn't seem to notice his reaction as she turned around and started talking about how he and Amy would get together. "You go to her office and ask her to redesign your new place. She comes over, and you talk all about the apartment's look and feel. She will ask about what you want it to feel like. Talk about the apartment thus turns into talk about you, then her, then coffee to dinner and then why are you staring at me like that?" Lei Lei had wandered the empty apartment as she talked before turning around to Jack's face still crumpled up in confusion.

"Don't you think you're going a little too fast?" he asked, "I mean, I think she's cool, but I don't want her to get in the way of our time together," he lied. Jack wasn't falling for Amy, but Thomas was. Or at least he thought.

Lei Lei laughed. "Don't worry, we will find time to screw around when my husband is busy." She walked closer and wrapped her arms around his waist. "I always enjoyed being a side girl."

Jack faked a smile and leaned down to kiss her, still confused by the situation, but her lips helped the confusion to fade. Relief filled his mind that his true feelings for Amy didn't jeopardize his relationship with Lei Lei and the information he could get from her. A piece of his mind did wander to the realization that he was the man that was having an affair with a married woman.

Chapter 26

Family Withdraw

Huan unlocked the front door of the bank in the early morning. The street was quiet like always; only a handful of cabs and cars drove past the bank. Once inside, the banker turned off the silent alarm and walked to his office, passing the glass tables with deposit slips and the silver counter with computers that stretched in front of a large wall-sized painting of an Asian countryside with an ancient Asian style house and family. In contrast, Huan's office was a simple place. Pictures of his wife and daughter sat on his desk. A small Buddhist statue, from his mother, looked at the empty, rarely-occupied seats facing his desk. He logged into his computer. A picture of him standing in front of the Forbidden City appeared as his wallpaper. He paid no mind to it as he fell into his routine: check who was coming in, all appointments that were being held, and filtering through loans. But before all that, he checked his emails, starting with business emails first full of memos and announcements, followed by his personal emails filled with ads and spam, and ending with his private email. This private email had never received or sent out any mail in the ten years he had worked at the bank. But it did have one drafted email today. He sat up in his chair, not even being able to remember the last time he saw a drafted email in this private account. Huan opened it.

'32' was the only thing it said. Huan checked the last time the draft was edited. 30 minutes ago. He deleted the draft, and left his office. He walked briskly to the breaker box and switched off the power to the fire exit in the bank and the vault. He went to the emergency exit in the back and checked his watch. Less than a minute. He looked up at the security camera. No light illuminated from the tiny bulb under the lens.

A knock came from the door. He held his breath as he pressed on the red handle. The only sound that followed were footsteps as four masked men walked through the door carrying two duffle bags each. They all wore black clothing except for their masks, which were colorful Chinese opera masks. As the last masked man came in, he gave a bow to Haun and said, "We need to make a withdrawal."

Huan bowed in return and lead them to the vault. "You only have fifteen minutes till the guards get here," Huan said, unlocking the safe and opening it to reveal several piles of cash, unaccounted for by the bank's system.

"Then get to work," said the leader handing a bag to Huan, and the five of them set to work stuffing it all into duffle bags. No words were spoken for the entire time. Once the bags were stuffed, they all gave the vault a final check, making sure all the cash was collected.

"Why does the Red Dragon need to make a withdrawal?" asked Huan, checking his watch to see they had a few minutes before the security office checked in. Huan looked up to see the masked leader swinging a nakiri knife into Haun's neck, knocking him to the floor. Haun pressed his hands against his neck to stop the flood of blood pouring from it. The masked leader stood silently, as if thinking of something to say, but said nothing before striking Huan in the neck again, though it caused more damage to Huan's fingers than the neck. After a few more attacks and the other robbers watching in silent, the leader stopped. He lifted his mask and spat on Huan, and left the vault as his companions closed the door.

Huan's body was not discovered until the security guard arrived two hours late due to his alarm clock not going off. By the time he got there, Huan had already bled out.

Chapter 27

Evening Trust

Jack sat on the floor of his new, empty apartment, gazing out his wall-sized window. The Hong Kong lights shined into his apartment illuminating the dark place. He was thinking of the size of shades he would need to keep out the night lights when he heard a soft tap of hollow metal on the floor.

"How long have you been here?" Jack asked, looking back to the assassin with the metal Jō. He wore the same apparel as when he attacked Lóng. His face was covered in the similar fashion from that night. Jack could still see some blood on it from his forehead; his scar was still visible, but healing well. The assassin sat on the floor beside Jack and leaned his Jō staff against his bare shoulder. Though the only light illuminating the room was from the skyscrapers and electronic billboards, Jack was still able to see the assassin's scars a lot better than last time. Small puncture scars near vital blood vessels seemed out of place with the multiple bullet and knife scars, and possibly some bite marks.

"I have a couple of extra shirts if you need one," Jack stated, hoping to ease the tension. The assassin remained silent, looking over the city. Jack took another sip of his beer.

"What happened?" asked the assassin in a voice so muffled Jack almost didn't hear it.

"Some former Red Pole decided to hit the bank we had some reserves in," said Jack. "I'm not sure how much, but I think it is in the millions. Lóng wasn't happy either. They even killed the insider we had so I hear."

"Lóng?"

"He's returning finally, I think he's got a new safe house for himself and his siblings. Not sure where yet, but enough about robberies and triads. Let's talk about something we both want to talk about." Jack placed his hand under his chin and looked up to the assassin.

"How can I trust you?" the assassin asked.

Jack rolled his head off his hand and made a loud huff like a child. "I don't know. You apparently trust me a little bit, or you wouldn't even be here. So, let me ask you this, why do you trust me?"

The assassin took a heavy breath. Jack took another sip of his beer and waited. "I don't know," said the assassin as he lowered his head in thought, before saying, "Running out of people to trust."

"You and me both."

They sat in silence as a thousand different words went through Jack's head to say, but all the words felt wrong. Mallory always said he talked too much, that sometimes the right thing to say is nothing.

"You remind me of a man," the assassin finally said. "A Swiss that some thought caused a lot of harm."

"What was his name?" Jack asked as hope built in him. He only knew one Swiss.

"Golay," answered the assassin. "But I'm not some. Do you know him?"

"I did," Jack smiled, remembering Amsterdam. The assassin's eyes frowned at the past tense words.

Their eyes met as they found something better than a common enemy. A common friend.

"My name is Guòqù," said the assassin.

"Interesting name. My name is Jack. Want to talk about them?" Jack asked softly.

Guòqù nodded and said, "What do you know about them?"

"I'm aware that their reach is global," said Jack. "They have a local agent to collect money from the crime leaders, sort of an extortioner of extortioners. They don't want to be known and will do anything to keep it that way. They also have some connections to politicians and the press to hide their involvement. Most of this is assumption, mind you, but some is from actual experience." Memories of the attack arose in his mind.

"Your assumptions are not too far off." Guòqù's words were quick and casual, taking Jack aback by the confidence Guòqù spoke in. "Agents are few and far between nowadays. Politicians and reporters don't know who's bribing them, but they are far from being just extortioners. They are also suppliers. They own the majority of the opium fields in the Golden Triangle and the Golden Crescent. The vast majority of slave trafficking is run through them." Tia stopped. His eyes fell to the floor.

"How do you know?" asked Jack, watching Guòqù carefully.

Guòqù took a breath before slowly taking his mask off, unwrapping his face like a mummy. He revealed a large metal piece covering his mouth and coming under his chin almost like a sling for his jaw. The skin right above the metal was callus.

"Because I'm their creation."

Chapter 28

Lost Child of Hong Kong

Inspector Ko and Inspector Chiu were only two of the four people in the bank that night. The rest of the police officers were outside. The crowd and reporters had already moved on a few hours ago with most of the investigating officers. Ko and Chiu stood in the vault looking over the taped area where the body was. Dried blood laid in and around the outline. Ko compared the surroundings with the folder of pictures taken earlier that day.

"Thoughts?" asked Chiu, bringing out his notepad and pen.

"I don't know," answered Ko as he walked around the blood stain. "Triads don't usually kill their insiders at the place they work. In this case, it would be burning their chance at using this bank again. That is assuming it was done by the same triad that used the bank. I know we have suspected this bank to hold triad cash. Maybe a group of thugs just got wind of the cash in it."

Ko was uncertain with his words. He stopped looking at the blood stain and rubbed his eyes. Chiu put his notepad away and waited for Ko to look at him, his hands folded in front of him. Ko nodded in agreement, and they left the vault. They used the same path Huan took when he came to work that morning. They said goodnight to the police officers, and drove back to the station as Hong Kong dove deeper into the night. They said nothing the entire trip back, as if they were returning from Huan's funeral. Ko kept his eyes on Hong Kong as it passed by. He just looked out his window at the passing lights of stores and street lamps. A soft rain started to fall on the city, tears of mourning for one of her children lost to greed.

"Any news?" Chiu asked, breaking the silence.

Ko took a breath as Chiu slowed the car to a stop at a traffic light. "No, and it's slowly getting to the point where the only news that will arise will be a body."

"Sorry," Chiu said as the light turned green.

Ko shrugged his shoulders. "I hope they just find a body, for his wife's sake."

A few minutes later, Chiu pulled the car into the covered parking at the station and parked it in the back corner as it was the only place open. He turned the car off and put his hand on the handle, but stopped when Ko started to talk again.

"We were foolish in thinking it was over, ignoring the petty crimes that didn't stop, pulling men and resources from the front lines, giving them space to breathe. And this is the result: blood starting to pour back into the streets, money gathering up dirt, and my brother's death."

Ko stopped talking to calm himself. He took a breath and continued. "We need to stop it, deliver justice to the triad again and fast, because I have a feeling we are dealing with a lot more triads than the last time, triads that are starting to bump into each other more violently."

They looked out the damp windshield in silence as they both dissected Ko's words. He turned and looked Chiu in the eyes. "We need evidence."

Chapter 29

New Boat

The speedboat raced toward the rising sun. Even with his thick sunglasses, the driver still found it a tad difficult to make out the yacht on the horizon. Below deck, Li sat in the little hatch on the hollow seats where cocaine and other illegal drugs would be stashed. Li adjusted his hoodie, as part of it got stuck to his bandages. Though he didn't require any more assistance, the stitches still bothered him. He counted the days till they could be removed. Nine to be precise.

The boat made a full turn. Li caught himself against the opposite wall, hissing in inconvenient pain at the fast movement of his arms. He wiped the dirt off his hands with his jeans as he felt the boat slow down. The hatch door opened. The driver and another one of Lóng's guards stood at the opening. The speedboat swayed under the shadow of the yacht. A ladder emerged from the side of the bigger ship. Li slowly climbed up the ladder, pausing only a brief moment when a wave caused both ships to shift. Guards, loaded with semi-automatic pistols under their sport coats, stood on deck. They bore a strange resemblance to a secret service team, but the tattoos threw it off. Li followed a guard with a neck tattoo of a snake inside the yacht where he found his siblings.

"I like the new crib," commented Li. The walls were a dark oak with the portholes covered with small, dark green drapes. A large poker table stood in the middle of the space surrounded by leather chairs where Lei Lei sat at. Lóng bent over in front of an open refrigerator under the bar at the far end of the room, its white light shining brighter than the dimmer yellow lights around the chamber and showing the lines under his eyes.

"Want a beer?" asked Lóng.

"Do you even have to ask?" answered Li.

Lóng pulled an off-brand beer out and handed it to Li. He opened it and took a sip as he sat down in the caddy corner from Lei Lei. Li choked. Once recovered, he said, "I still don't see how you like this stuff."

"It's cheap and good," said Lóng. He slumped down with them.

"If you can call piss good," Li said, but then took another sip.

"Then don't drink it," said Lóng, his voice mellow and tired. He took another sip of his own beer as Li and Lei Lei watched him. He continued, "How much do you all know?"

"We got robbed. How much?" asked Li.

"Too much of our clean money and our banker got killed."

Li's eyes widened; Lei Lei didn't react. "How?" was the only thing Li could get out.

"Someone on the inside," said Lóng. "Someone who knew the normal routine, because it looks like Huan let them in."

Li sat his beer on the table. "Damn, man." Lóng and Lei Lei were quiet. Li continued, "Any ideas on who it was?"

"Jack did cross my mind…"

Li bowed up. "You still don't trust him?"

"I didn't say it was, but you never know."

Li huffed in dissatisfaction as he slumped back in his chair. "You know it's more likely Boqin than anyone else."

"But how did he learn about the bank?" asked Lóng. "The process? He was a 49er when the cops came knocking. He wouldn't have known about it."

"That doesn't mean he couldn't have learned it from another Red Pole that left. And why aren't you applying that logic to Jack? He's a 49er too."

The bickering could have continued for a few hours if it weren't for Lei Lei interrupting it because of her boredom. "You're both wrong. Zemi is the one behind it, though I wouldn't be surprised if Boqin supported him."

"Zemi?" exclaimed Li. "How did Zemi know about the bank?"

"He's the former White Paper Fan's son. The one who was arrested and hung himself in his cell." Lei Lei filling Li in on the details of the things he missed during his prodigal son years. Li gulped at what happened to the last White Paper Fan.

"So," said Lóng, "Boqin isn't bold enough to do it himself but isn't scared enough to not support someone else to do it. Does this suggest they could be joining forces soon? Which means we need to be ready, which we may be."

Lóng didn't wait for an answer he didn't need. He stood up and walked out of the room. His siblings followed him through a tight hallway into the master bedroom with a king-sized bed taking up most of the space. Lóng pushed his hands into the bed like a knife into a cake and pushed outward, revealing a hidden compartment under the bed into which Lóng descended. Li followed him cautiously. Lei Lei followed also, but seemed unimpressed. The space below was dark. Barely tall enough for them to stand up straight, with only a few inches to spare for their heads. The room was wider than the room above it and longer. Li tried to touch the walls for guidance but couldn't find anything. Lóng turned on the light as Lei Lei stepped off the ladder. The light bounced off the heavy steel walls and was absorbed by the large wooden crates down the center of the room. The containers came to Lóng's elbows and were wider than the king-sized bed above, and stretched down the length of the ship. Lóng motioned to Li to get on the opposite side of the crate he was next to. They placed their fingers under the lid and slid it far enough for Lóng to reach in and pull out a brand-new submachine gun.

"Forty of these, sixty semi-automatic pistols, twenty shotguns, a handful of AKs, and enough ammo for all of them to make a warlord jealous. And that's just for this crate." Lóng puffed his chest out as he felt the gun in his fingers like a woman's hand. "If Boqin tries anything else aggressive, he'll wish he hadn't." Lóng's voice quivered at the end, followed by a cough. His phone rang before Li could pester him about it. "Hello? Yu, glad you called me back listen, I have a job for you."

Lóng climbed up the ladder, leaving Lei Lei and Li alone. Li walked around and looked into the open crate, observing the different firearms while Lei Lei was on her phone.

"Is this what he did for those two months away? Did he forget we just got robbed?" questioned Li.

"This was before the robbery, and he didn't need clean cash for this shopping spree," answered Lei Lei not looking up from her phone.

Li shook his head. "He was never the fighter when we were younger, he always had the ability to get along with the adults but just never with the other kids. He was even backing down from the younger kids."

Lei Lei lifted her head from her screen. "You're right, he isn't a fighter. If Dad died after the mole, Lóng would have been in a much better position to lead. He's a Dragon Head for keeping the status quo. Not for a change." She returned to her phone.

"Yeah, if he used his counsel we might be doing better. Having a full council would help, too."

"Thanks, prick," responded Lei Lei.

"At least you are able to help, I feel like all I do is just listen to what he would do if the mole didn't happen and talk about our childhood. Like, he didn't even consult me on any of this stuff, and I'm the guy that's supposed to handle the money!" Li's voice shifted from sincere to angry. "At least you're not worthless!" He hit the crate. Lei Lei looked back up from her phone at Li as he just stared at the box.

"He still sees you as the little brother that left us," said Lei Lei. "He sees you as a symbol of a better time. Also getting sliced up by Boqin didn't help. And he didn't approve of Jack taking the lead in the talks with Chi."

"Well, I didn't know Boqin had become a bastard while I was gone, and why doesn't he trust Jack? He brought the rat literally to his doorstep and saved his life. And my life twice! And so, what if he took over the talks? We got Chi in the end."

Lei Lei placed her phone in her pocket and waited till Li looked her in the eye. "That rat did a lot more damage than just getting half our men arrested. If this were earlier, Lóng would have trusted him by now, may have even made him a bodyguard. But the rat happened, and here we are." She opened her arms, displaying the area they stood in. Li looked around at the bare walls that kept them from the sea.

"What should we do then?" Li asked.

Lei Lei shrugged in response. "Help him and try at all cost to stay out of war.

Chapter 30

Coping Love

Jack twirled Amy's business card in his fingers as he rode the elevator to her office floor. Collection money from that morning filled his pockets. The digital counter changed as he passed each floor. He closed his eyes and breathed slowly, and his thoughts fell back to Mallory.

"This is stupid," he said to himself in the empty elevator. "I hate feelings. Why am I wasting my time with this hope of something? I have to find The Twelve."

The elevator doors opened to a young man sitting at a glass desk and dressed like he just stepped off a fashion runway. Jack felt quite dull for the first time in a long time.

"What can I do for you, honey?" the man asked as Jack stepped out of the elevator.

"I'm looking for Amy's office?"

"Left, right, up the half-stairs then right past the turquoise moon but before the half-built man painting. Keep your phone out past the first desk but keep it hidden past the second one. Then go behind the green-colored steel column, and you're there." He went back to his slim computer as Jack stood there bewildered.

"I'm sorry, but could you show me?" Jack asked looking down on him.

The man shrugged his shoulders. "Sure."

He stood up and proceeded down the path he described. The painting of the half man was a little more literal than Jack thought it would be. He followed his guide's lead and kept his phone out past the first secretary who was in her twenties and talking the ear off of a client. The second secretary was older and had her nose in a romance novel. Jack and his guide rounded a corner where the floor opened up. Large architect desks were sparsely spread out around the floor, all with personal items each hinting of the desks' occupants. Four glass offices sat at the corners of the space, with a colored column at the corner nearest to the center. Jack stopped walking as his heart sped up a little and his hands grew clammy. A young woman carrying rolled up papers bumped into the man Jack was following. She almost dropped her papers as she spun to keep them in her arms, though Jack saw her falling as the old Glass base burned around her. Jack shook his head and started walking again. He blinked a few times to help him focus on the place he was in at the moment, and not on the one a continent away that had been underground. Walking toward the office at the far-right corner behind the green column, Jack was able to see Amy at her desk drawing on a pure white piece of paper.

"Found this guy looking for you," said the man.

"Hey, thanks," said Amy, looking up from her sketches of a nightingale. The man let Jack in and was gone before the door closed. Amy stood up from her simple, white office chair. She gave Jack a hug, and Jack felt his tension from earlier melt away.

"How are you doing?" she said. "What made you come by today? Please have a seat. Do you want some tea?"

"I'm good, but thanks for the offer." Jack sat down in a black bowl-like chair across from her that was surprisingly comfy.

"So, what is the reason for this visit?" asked Amy as she poured herself a cup of tea.

"I came by for some advice."

"Oh really?" She sat back down in her chair. "What advice do you need?"

"Well, I've finally found my own place and need some help with it."

Amy took a sip of her tea from her black-and-white striped mug. "What kind of help?"

"Just help with picking out some furniture and colors."

"Okay. What kind of place?"

"A loft downtown."

Her left eyebrow raised slightly. "Really? You know, living in industrial lofts runs you the risk of getting you in trouble with the law right?"

"I do. This isn't industrial, though, so no worries."

She nodded. "Ok, how big is it?"

"About two thousand square feet."

She put down her mug as both eyebrows went up this time. "That's big. You sure it isn't industrial?"

Jack chuckled. "That's what the owner said. If it would make you feel more comfortable about it, do you want to come by and check it out? Maybe after lunch with me?"

Amy tilted her head as a small smile appeared on her face. "Sure, I don't see why not. But I pick."

Jack nodded in surprise that his cheesy pickup line actually worked. "I would prefer it that way. Friday sounds good?" Jack asked, smiling as his phone vibrated.

"Sounds perfect, I'll meet you downstairs at eleven?"

Jack silenced his phone. "Friday, eleven, downstairs, got it."

Jack's phone vibrated again. He ignored it, but Amy heard it.

"Here," she said, "let me write down my personal number while you tend to your phone. It seems like someone really needs you."

"I doubt it. Probably just a funny picture."

Jack pulled his phone out of his gray pants. He had two missed calls and a text from Li. The text read: "Yu's dead. Lóng wants to talk."

Chapter 31

Cheap Date

"So Heng is really meeting with the Red Dragon Head today?" a teenage boy asked Yong as they got into an old SUV.

"Not the Head, just their Sandal. Here, keep this in your pocket." Yong handed the short fifteen-year-old a spring-loaded pocket knife.

"Just a rep? If anyone is going to send a rep, it should be us."

Yong slapped the kid on the back of the head before starting the car. "If you want to get far in the triad, kid, you need to first know your place. The Red Dragon is a pure triad, we aren't."

The child turned red. "But Heng said we are just as strong…"

"Heng says a lot of bullshit."

The boy leaned back to observe Yong as he drove through the busy streets. "But you're Heng's Deputy, his right…"

Yong cut him off again. "No, I'm not. I'm just a 49er that does what he is told and keeps his mouth shut, which you should too."

The kid took his advice for the rest of the drive.

After ten minutes, Yong pulled into a construction site. The lack of workers gave it a haunted feeling. The dark clouds sprinkling added to the mood. The two took the elevator to the twentieth floor, seeing no one the whole way until they reached their floor. Two twins, Tin and Tan, dressed similar to Yong and the kid - sports coats with a t-shirt - met them. Yong greeted with a bow, and Yong and the boy followed the twins through a maze of steel beams, workbenches, and a plastic sheet imitating a door to a room. Two chairs were set up on opposite sides of a small cards table. A single light illuminated the room from the ceiling.

"This will work well," said Yong, "Where are the refreshments?"

"In here," said Tan. He pushed a plastic tarp aside and brought out an ice chest and opened it to show the contents of it. A bottle of wine with cheese and crackers. Yong shook his head.

"He wanted this?" asked Yong.

Tan nodded.

"He's losing his roots," Yong added.

They set up the table with the imported snacks and plastic cups. To a newcomer, it resembled more of a romantic cheap date rather than a meeting of organized criminals. It wasn't long till Heng arrived. He took a seat that faced him toward the entrance of the room, with Yong, Tin, Tan, and the kid positioned at the corners. Heng's features resembled a Buddha in a suit. He ate some of the cheese and tasted the wine, all imports from Europe. Heng sat silent for thirty minutes, playing on his phone until the Straw Sandal finally arrived. Yu was dressed in a suit similar to Heng, only lacking two-hundred pounds. Heng didn't stand when Yu entered. He gestured to the chair opposite of him as he put his phone away and took a bite of the cheese.

"I'm so glad you were able to meet with me, the Dragon Head sends his regards as he is unable to attend," started Yu.

Heng swallowed his cheese. "Understandable, being a coward takes a lot of time."

Yu's eyes pierced Heng, but the fat man took no notice of it. "He had pressing business matters to attend to."

"Of course," said Heng. "Now to our business. What is your proposal?"

"If it seems the appropriate time," said Yu, who shifted uneasily in his chair.

"It does," interrupted Heng. "Now get to the main point." The guard's faces stayed stone solid except for the kid, whose eyes betrayed excitement and confusion.

Yu recovered from the interruption with a softer voice. "The Dragon Head thinks it would be wise for you and your brothers to come back and join the Red Dragon."

Heng nodded his head and wiped his mouth with a handkerchief. He placed it back in his breast pocket, pulled out a small handgun from his jacket, and shot Yu in the face. Shock filled the kid's eyes as his dreams of what kind of work he would do for a triad were met with reality. Heng gestured to Tin and Tan to take the body out. They stood still for a moment, before proceeding to tip back the chair that Yu was sat in and carry him out in it. Yu's dead face glared up at Tan. Blood from the bullet hole dropped down on to Tan's pants as he walked backward out the door. Before leaving entirely, Tan looked back. Heng drank his wine with the kid in one corner frightened and Yong in the other corner staring back at Tan, shaking his head. When Heng finished his glass of wine, he stood up with a huff and gave orders.

"Yong, you stay and clean up."

"Yes, sir."

Yong motioned to the kid to follow Heng. The child's eyes were still wide in fear, but he nodded and slowly followed Heng, staring at the blood trail Yu's body left as they walked out. Yong got to work picking up the food and wine. When he was finished with that, Tin and Tan returned.

"Did you know?" asked Tin.

Yong shook his head. "No, I take it you all didn't either?"

They shook their heads too.

Yong placed the ice chest on the table. "What did you do with the body?"

"Wrapped it up in a plastic tarp," answered Tan. "Want us to dump it in the sea?"

Yong tapped his fingers on the ice chest. "This is too far," he finally said.

"You think?" Tin and Tan said in unison.

Yong gave a smile. "I do." His smile disappeared as fast as it came. "His recklessness and stupidity are going to get us all arrested or killed. Most likely the latter with this new stunt."

They stood in silence for a minute as Yong kept staring at Yu's blood on the floor.

"What are we going to do?" asked Tan. "Leave?"

"No," answered Yong. "We are going to change it."

Chapter 32

A Member Short

Jack hustled up the stairs to the second floor of the gym, the day far from over. He opened the door to all the eyes in the upstairs room staring at him. Small tables and chairs filled the room, all facing the mounted TV on the wall with Lóng on it. The TV was used more for movies and sports than business meetings. All of the Red Dragon's Red Poles were there with their right-hand men and bodyguards. Lei Lei and Li were in the front near the TV with a younger man sitting on the floor, laptop connected to the TV, webcam pointed to the crowd.

"Jack, I'm glad you're here. Did Li fill you in?" asked Lóng,

Jack could tell he was trying to keep it calm and collected. "All I know is Yu is dead," answered Jack, folding his hands behind him and giving a small bow toward Lóng.

"That…That is correct. He was meeting with Heng about joining us yesterday, and one of our establishments find him in our dumpster. Shot in the head."

"Do we know who did it?" asked Jack.

"Boqin or Heng," stated Lei Lei.

"What about Zemi?" asked Jack.

"He's a puppet for Boqin, so if he did it, it would have been Boqin who made the call," said Chi, looking already more confident than the first time Jack met him.

"Either way," said Lóng, taking control of the conversation sternly, "I want the bastard dead. That is why you're here Jack. I want to know who did it, who pulled the trigger, and I want them dead."

"What if it was Boqin or…" one of the Red Poles begin to ask.

"Dead!" shouted Lóng, interrupting him. Lóng's face was red, and his veins popped when he made the order. "Dead in two weeks!"

The feed cut out, and the young technician started to pack his things. The Red Poles and their companions started to slowly trickle out. They cast glances at Jack as he stood next to the door, waiting for them all to leave. Once they were all out, Jack started to ask his questions.

"Besides Lóng being pissed, what else did I miss?" He walked up to Lei Lei and Li.

"Not much, just the small details about the new shipment of guns and keeping our eyes open," answered Lei Lei as she sat down at one of the tables. Li stared at the laptop and the last bit of accessories being packed up by the young man. "He really wants Yu's death avenged, like tomorrow," added Lei Lei, folding her arms.

"I could see that. Did we find anything helpful on the body?"

"Just this: no one has taken responsibility for it, but it's still early." Lei Lei handed Jack a ziplock baggy with a blood-covered map of the Landmark Central Mall and a coin. A date and time were written on it at one of the fountains. The IT guy left with his second-hand bag and expensive laptop. Jack, Lei Lei and Li were the last ones left in the room.

"Do we still have the body?" asked Jack.

"Yeah," answered Lei Lei, sitting down at the closest table.

"What if we got our contact in the Police Force to 'find' the body? They could investigate who wrote the note." Jack used his fingers for air quotes when he mentioned 'find.' He sat down with Lei Lei while Li still stood against the dirty red wall, looking at the floor.

Lei Lei shook her head. "I don't want the cops snooping around. We could get into a lot of shit with that."

"But we could get a legitimate lead on the killer."

Lei Lei stood her ground, unmoved. "The man was one of Lóng's personal bodyguards before he made him his Straw Sandal. I don't want to give them any reason to look into us."

"Okay." Jack backed down, not wanting to get Lei Lei heated up against him. "Want me to follow this lead?" Jack asked, holding up the baggy.

"Yeah. Be on your toes. It could be a trap. Heng was supposedly the last person to have seen him since he was meeting with him. Keep your eyes out for his goons."

"Okay. How does Lóng plan on talking to the rest of the wandering Red Poles?"

"Li and I will. Duyi, Tung, and Xing are still free agents. Still don't know where Tao is, and Gui is still in prison. Though Enlai may already be off the market since he's the older brother of Zemi."

"Tao will decide it," said Li. Lei Lei and Jack looked at Li as he finally spoke. His voice was soft and meek. "Where Tao places his loyalty, that is the side that will have the upper hand."

"You're right. However, we need to take care of the others first," added Lei Lei. "Jack, I want you to find Yu's killer. Be careful, though, if you talk to Heng's men. I have a feeling he could be a part of it, if not the actual killer."

"Understood."

Lei Lei continued, "And Li and I will take care of the Red Poles. I will get someone else to check on Enlai to see if he's already with Boqin."

Lei Lei and Jack stood up. Li slowly leaned off the wall. "Li," said Lei Lei, "can you get the car? I want to have a word with Jack for a second." Lei Lei seductively wrapped her arms around Jack. Li showed the first sign of an expression that whole night. It was similar to a child when their parents kiss.

"At least wait till I get outside." He quickly walked out as Jack chuckled under his breath. Once the door was closed, Lei Lei let go of Jack, and her professionalism was back.

"I also have two other things I need you to do."

"Ok." Jack took a half a step back and crossed his arms.

"Li has taken Yu's death hard."

"I can tell. He seems a little out of it."

"I know, that is why I am going to send him to Lóng for a bit. They will need each other to get through this."

"Ok, so will you take care of the Red Poles yourself?"

"Yes. What I need from you is to pack up some of his personal stuff and drop it off here. I'm going to send him to meet with Lóng today."

Jack nodded his head. "I can do that, what's the other thing?"

"Your cop." Lei Lei walked over to the back of the room where the teapot sat on the counter.

"What about him?" Jack said, thinking about Fu and Guòqù.

"Are you his only connection?" Lei Lei filled a kettle with water.

"Yeah, just like Ink told me to," answered Jack.

"Good, I want you to give me all the stuff you have on him. Family, how you get a hold of him, everything." She placed the kettle on the pot burner, plugging it in. "As things are getting more unstable, we will need to be able to react to things quickly, and you may be busy on an errand for me." She turned the stove on and turned around. "Is that all right?" Though phrased as a question, Jack knew it was an order.

"Sure." A knot started to form inside of Jack's stomach.

Lei Lei turned back to the counter and took a box of tea bags out of a drawer and placed one in her mug. "Good."

"You know," added Jack, slowly walking toward her, placing his hands in his pockets. "I still can't put my finger on you. I've seen a fun side of you, a playful, carefree side, and now here's all this business side. I guess I'm just having trouble trying to figure out which side is the real you?"

Lei Lei faced Jack, her eyebrow raised and a smile formed at the corner of her mouth. "Who gives a damn which one is the real me?" The kettle whistled.

Chapter 33

Therapy Session

Mallory lay beside Thomas, gazing into his eyes as the morning sun rose behind him. She wore a white tank top with her blonde hair in a ponytail behind her. She smiled at him as if he had just said a cheesy pickup line. She slowly reached out to him. She placed her soft hand on his lips. Puckering her lips like she was about to kiss him, she shushed him instead with a low, muffled voice. Thomas woke up and saw Guòqù bent over him with his hand over Thomas's mouth, making the shushing sound.

"We need to talk," Guòqù whispered as he slowly lifted his rough hand off of Jack's mouth.

"Why are you whispering? Are The Twelve employing insects now?"

Guòqù didn't laugh. He stepped back and sat down on the floor, out of view of the city's lights. Jack sat up with his back against the wall.

"You said I can get close to him?" asked Guòqù in a muffled voice through his steel mouthpiece.

"You can. Li has left to spend some time with Lóng. I was ordered to pick up his stuff and drop it off at the gym tomorrow." Jack looked at the clock beside his bed on the floor. "Today, I mean."

Guòqù was silent. He placed his Jō against his head as if he was going to gain some new information from it. "How will I follow it?"

"Just follow it. They will probably ship it to a P.O. box where someone else will pick it up. Then follow them. That's sort of your forte - the stalking thing."

"Are you done?" said Guòqù, annoyed.

"Sorry, just trying to keep our spirits high."

"My spirit will be high when I find The Twelve and kill them all."

"Why?" Jack leaned forward. "Did they do…" Jack moved his hand over his mouth, "… that to you?"

Guòqù looked at the floor, his grip on his Jō tightening. "No, I have reasons just like you. Does it matter if you know them?"

"It would help."

"Help who?"

"Both of us!" Jack shouted. He stopped and lowered his voice. "We both have some heavy baggage, okay? Some deep scars that we have to keep hidden behind a costume that sometimes feels like a million pounds pressing down on you every day. And you know it doesn't go away when you sleep. It just lays there, pressing on your chest." Jack stopped and closed his eyes as he leaned back against the wall. "I…I just want some help with my bags, man. I need some help with this to accurately contribute to bringing down The Twelve." Jack's voice left him as if he'd just finished a marathon. He breathed slowly, realizing how hard it was to keep it all together without a handler or Mallory.

Guòqù leaned against the wall as well for a few seconds in silence, before speaking. "I can do that," he muttered.

Thomas took a deep breath through his mouth and told Guòqù everything: about Amsterdam, his first mission, Golay, his first kill, the pimp, the teenage girls, Mallory, and Spain. Guòqù sat and listened carefully for several hours, reacting to nothing, not interrupting once.

"Better?" asked Guòqù after Thomas was all done.

Jack clenched his jaw, wiping the few tears he had collected. "Yeah, I'm great now."

"It will get better when they are dead." Guòqù stood up with the help of his Jō.

"Will it?" asked Jack sincerely.

Guòqù stood. "You need sleep. What time are you going to drop off the stuff?"

Jack looked at the clock. "Two."

Guòqù nodded and walked out of Jack's bedroom, closing the door behind him. Jack settled back into his bed and stared out at Hong Kong. He drifted to sleep with thoughts of the end of this journey, wondering if twelve deaths would cure him of the pain, wondering why he was doing all this, wondering if he was seeking justice or merely blood. Wondering if he could drop being Jack and simple be Thomas again.

Chapter 34

Room A

Inspector Ko sat in his office, staring at his computer screen, reading over the report of the bank robbery for the twentieth time. By scrolling over every picture his men took and links to the security videos, he had the file memorized by now. He reread the emails and texts the former banker had on all his devices. He leaned back and rubbed his eyes as Inspector Chiu walked in.

"Minute?" asked Chiu.

Ko nodded. Chiu shut the door behind him and sat down in the seat beside him. "The bank?"

"Yes," Ko answered in guilt. "I have to say, this is one of the cleanest jobs I've ever seen. The banker must have been the insider, but nothing is turning up."

Chiu nodded in empathy.

"So?" asked Ko.

Chiu handed him a folder. Inside was a promotion form for Fu. Ko sighed heavily, as it had all the signatures it needed besides his. Ko took a pen and signed it as Chiu said, "Kill a runner and bring another in and you get promoted by the chief.

In our day you had to earn your honor instead of stumbling upon it." Ko slid the folder back to Chiu who remarked, "The other one didn't even give us anything."

Ko opened up the interrogation report, short and empty, and dragged his mouse up to close the preview of the report. He stopped when he caught the name of the interrogating officer.

"Kaoru?" Ko asked with surprise. Chiu showed the same expression. Ko checked the status of the prisoner. "He's still in the holding cells. Let's go."

Ko stood up with force and left his office, muttering under his breath, "That soft bastard and his soft voice and weird questions won't help with these low life grunts."

Chiu was close behind him. They marched quickly through the station to the holding cell's desk. Ko ordered the officer at the desk to move the runner to the oldest and his favorite interrogation room. They didn't have to wait long until Kaoru walked in.

"Hello, Ko and Chiu, what are you old triad hunters up to?" Kaoru's voice was high and whiny.

"Just trying to fix the damage you've done," Ko responded in a low tone.

Kaoru's head moved back as he folded his lotioned hands over his chest. "What?"

"The bus extortion case? Your report was shit."

Kaoru's eyes went wide as he opened his mouth in shock. "Well, I'm sorry if he didn't have much to say at the moment."

"So you just filed it with no follow-up?"

"Yeah, he didn't have much to say because he confessed to it up front."

"Who put you on this case?" Ko asked with his hands in his pocket.

"Fu requested me because he didn't have the rank to question him."

The officer returned and informed Ko that the suspect was in the room. Ko thanked the officer coldly and told Karou before leaving, "Figures. Lucky idiots like brown-nosing."

Interrogation Room A was Ko's favorite because of the many successful breaks he'd had with it. It was a dirty concrete room with two rusty steel chairs bolted to the ground facing each other. Here memories were made. No lamp, no table, not even a see-through mirror. It was this room that Ko gained vital information from a drug runner that helped his brother and other international police officers gain access to infiltrate the triad those many years ago. He hoped he'd be as lucky this time.

When they reached the room, the prisoner was already there, seated and handcuffed to the chair with an officer stationed by the thick oak door. Ko and Chiu gave the officer their guns, and he left the room with the weapons, closing the heavy door behind him. The prisoner wore an orange jumpsuit with no socks or shoes. Ko could see a tattoo of a flame popping out of the inmate's clothes on the back of his neck. Ko circled him with Chiu in the corner. Ko sat in the other chair facing the prisoner, who looked as if this was his hundredth time. The prisoner's hair was buzzed off, and his left eyebrow was missing. Ko focused on the prisoner for a minute in silence. The prisoner looked back, bored. Ko checked his watch. Chiu unplugged the security camera in the corner of the room. The prisoner wasn't bored anymore as the little red dot turned off.

"I only want to know one simple thing, off the record."

The prisoner said nothing as he stared at Ko with fear in his eyes.

"Do you work for the Red Dragon?" Ko asked

The prisoner's fear melted away as disrespect replaced it. "Don't insult me."

"Ok, who do you work for? And don't give me that you're your own boss bullshit. Dragon Heads don't do the job of lonely worthless grunts like you."

The inmate's face grew red. "You don't know me. I'm different."

Ko rolled his eyes and leaned back. "Of course you are. You are a unique little butterfly." The prisoner started to speak, but Ko spoke over him. "Oh wait, this is the real world where 49ers are left in the gutter to rot."

"Don't you mean the Red Dragon, because that is where they are."

"Bitter that they didn't hire you when you were a pup?"

"They couldn't keep talent like me tied down. That's why I left, that is why everyone left. Now they are the ones in the gutter. They are the ones rotting!"

Ko walked to the door. Chiu plugged the security camera back in and quickly followed Ko back to his office. Chiu arrived as Ko pulled out the dry erase board that was pushed to the corner of the room since the mole. Chiu closed the door while Ko quickly wiped the board down with a paper towel as he explained.

"In the back of my mind, I had a fear this would happen. We only crippled the Red Dragon and left a huge void that is now being quickly filled by new, young triads. We are going to need to stamp this out before it gets out of hand." Ko stopped before he started writing on the board and looked at Chiu with excitement in his eye. "We need to talk to Su."

Chapter 35

Fountain Wishes

The hustle and bustle of the mall was almost too loud for Yong to hear his own thoughts, which was why he liked it. Glancing around, he could see Tin and Tan on the second floor that overlooked the fountain and the bench he sat on. Yong took a sip of his bubble tea and checked the time. His stomach tensed up as he saw it was a minute past twelve. Yu's head kicking back from the gunshot came to the forefront of Yong's mind. He knew that wouldn't be his fate if Heng found out what he was doing. No, Yong's death would take several weeks, days if Heng was kind. But Yong couldn't remember the last time Heng was kind. Those thoughts left his mind when he finally saw the Lumberjack.

The tall, bearded white man stuck out like a sore thumb. He was wearing a bright graphic shirt with dark jeans and a pair of aviators. Yong laughed to himself when he saw him. The Lumberjack walked up to the fountain and tossed a coin into it. Yong waited till the Lumberjack's head glanced in his direction before standing up and tossing a coin in the fountain, too. He sat back down on his bench, with the Lumberjack sitting on the bench next to his.

"I think we may not have needed the coin toss if I knew they were going to send you," commented Yong.

The Lumberjack chuckled under his breath. "I agree. I'm Jack."

"Nice to meet you. I'm Yong, Heng's right-hand man some would say."

Jack crossed his legs. "Impressive. So, I assume you know something about Yu's killer."

"I do indeed."

"And I take it you won't just tell me out of the kindness of your heart?"

"Maybe," Yong shrugged and added under his breath, "if the protection is right."

"I can promise that and more," Jack said. "I've been ordered to kill the man who pulled the trigger and honor those who help me with that."

"Well, Heng pulled the trigger. I was there." Yong looked at his hands, the hands that dumped the body in the dumpster. "I'm risking a lot coming here."

"I don't think you are. You planned on it not being that big of a risk," said Jack, stretching his arm out on the bench like Mallory was sitting beside him and listening to him pick someone else's lie apart for once. "Two personal bodyguards on the second floor. Smart."

Yong held his hands together on his lap. "I like to have a backup plan."

"That's good, smart of you. The Red Dragon likes their employees to be smart."

Yong looked straight at Jack.

Jack turned back toward him and said with a half-smile, "Tell me. How loyal are the men to you?"

"Very."

"Would they follow you if Heng stepped down?"

Yong looked back to the fountain. "Most would. The younger ones would have some difficulty."

"Would they cause a problem?" Jack watched a group of teenagers approach the fountain to throw their wishes in.

Yong pushed out his bottom lip and shook his head. "No, it would be a good experience for them."

"Good. When can I talk to Heng?"

"He's away for 'personal reasons,' but I can get him back,"

"Good." Jack stood up and brushed a few wrinkles out of his shirt. "Inform your closest friends, get your affairs in order, and I will meet your former employer when appropriate."

Jack walked away, passing the group of teenagers laughing together as one of the girls threw a wish over the fountain. Yong started calling his trusted friends, not giving a thought to the excitement and fear growing inside him that he would be a Red Pole in the morning.

Chapter 36

Road Rage

Tiě watched the gym from the roof of a three-story building next door. He laid completely still on his stomach, with his head just peering over the edge, studying the back of the gym. He wore his usual attire, but with a new black long-sleeved shirt that he had stolen from the back of a delivery truck. His headscarf was wrapped tightly around his head, leaving only a small slot for his eyes to see. His Jō was strapped to his back and moved slightly up and down with his breathing. His body stopped. His eyes narrowed as a new black car drove up to the back of the gym. Two men in suits with guns protruding from under their jackets stepped out and walked up the fire escape and disappeared through the second-floor door. Guòqù pushed himself up slightly but stopped as the door opened again and the two men came out with a duffle bag. Once the men were in the car, Guòqù got up and slowly followed them on the roof as they drove forward and turned right onto the main street. Guòqù ran to the opposite side of the building and jumped down, catching the second story fire escape and jumping off it to the alleyway below, where an old motorcycle sat with a black helmet that Guòqù quickly put on, covering his entire head.

He revved up the bike and drove out of the alley in pursuit of the black car. He quickly spotted them two cars in front of him. They took a right further into Hong Kong. Guòqù sped up and passed the two cars between them on the sidewalk. The pedestrians took zero notice of him.

For the next several blocks, Guòqù had no difficulty in following them, keeping a good thirty feet or a car behind them. As they grew closer to the outer edge of the business district, traffic became incredibly slow as more cars filled the road. The sidewalk was packed with pedestrians, food stands, and a couple of musicians. Hitting a red-light, Guòqù kept his eyes locked on the car as it sat a car ahead of him at the intersection.

Guòqù let go of his bike and stretched out his hands when he heard the faint sound of a couple of motorcycles coming up behind him through the stopped traffic. They grew louder. He saw one of the pedestrians step out of the crowd toward the black car. The two bikes stopped beside him; the cyclists were dressed in white undershirts with tattooed arms and similar helmets to Guòqù except for the paintings of dragons on them. The pedestrian beside the car took the duffle bag from the passenger and disappeared into the crowd down the intersecting street. Guòqù slowly tried to follow him, but the motorcyclist with tattooed flames on his arm blocked his path as he stared him down. Guòqù kept the other motorcyclist behind him in his vision with his side mirror.

"I wouldn't do that, man," said the rider blocking his path. The one behind him kicked out his kickstand and got off his bike while reaching into his pocket. "Dangerous for the pedestrians."

Guòqù saw the motorcyclist behind him coming closer and pulling his hand out of his jacket pocket with a knife. An average man wouldn't have noticed that action. Guòqù grabbed his Jō and pulled it down with one hand while the other hand unclipped it from his back. The Jō's other end flew up and hit the motorcyclist behind him in the jaw before his hand was completely out of his pocket. The helmet visor cracked as the rider fell back, dazed. Guòqù kept the Jō moving over his shoulder and toward the rider in front of him, knocking him off his bike before he even knew what had happened.

Guòqù jumped onto the motorcycle in front of him and drove after the man with the duffle bag. His path was quickly blocked as the black car opened its door and the passenger stepped out with a handgun and a ski mask on. Guòqù sped up. He ran straight into the gunman and ran him into the open door. It broke, as well as the gunman's ribs. Guòqù used his free hand to hold down the gun and pressed his Jō on the man's throat. Guòqù glanced to his right to see the man with the duffle bag getting on the back of another bike.

A gunshot rang from the inside of the car at the same moment Guòqù felt the sting of a bullet, but not for the first time. Guòqù pulled the pinned man down between him and the shooting driver, and he absorbed the next two shots in the shoulder for Guòqù. He ripped the gun out of the loose hand and fired four shots as the driver tried to escape the car, but instead fell through the open door. The crowd by now had gone into complete panic as they all scattered away from the scene. Guòqù looked back for the runner, but saw no evidence of him in the mob. Guòqù heard the faint sound of sirens as his human shield tried to struggle. Guòqù hit him on the back of the head, and the body went limp. He pulled the unconscious body onto his motorcycle, revealing a bullet hole in his leg. Guòqù used the strap of his Jō to keep the limp man's arms around him. He lifted his leg to see blood on the other side, and the bullet lodged into one of the metal bars on the motorcycle. Guòqù drove away from the sound of the sirens. He took sidewalks and dirty alleyways toward the edge of Hong Kong. For the first time in a long time, he smiled under his metal jaw.

Chapter 37

Yellow Tape

"The ink from his promotion isn't even dry, and he's already here assisting in the investigation of Hong Kong's first public shooting in years." Ko's words hissed through his teeth as he walked past the yellow tape and toward the scene of the crime. Chiu following silently behind him, pad and pen in hand. "It's bullshit," said Ko as he walked behind Fu, who stood behind another officer taking a picture of the car and the dead body on the other side. Fu was wearing a new suit; the light blue color seemed brighter next to Ko's dark gray suit. "What do we have?" demanded Ko to Fu.

"A shooting, sir," responded Fu respectfully.

"No shit, I want to know what happened."

"Yes sir. What we have gotten so far from the scene and eyewitnesses is that a biker a car behind assaulted two other bikers, then charged the passenger of this car, shot the driver, and kidnapped the passenger. A few think they saw the assaulting biker get shot, so I was planning on getting samples of all the blood spots."

Ko walked around the car and kneeled over the dead body. His frustration subsided as he focused on the task at hand. The blood further from the body was completely dry, though the body still was slowly bleeding. Ko snapped his fingers, and Chiu quickly placed a pen in his bare fingers. Ko took the pen and with it pushed the dead man's collar down. Ko didn't have much trouble making out the dragon tattoo through the blood and bullet holes.

"No license plate, I assume?" asked Ko, a hint kinder than before.

"Correct," answered Fu.

"Fu, I need you to keep the press out of this, alright?"

"I can do that sir."

"When they ask you what happened, you tell them it was a homicide and only a homicide."

Fu nodded, eyeing the dead body and its tattoos before walking toward the police line, where a few bystanders were gathering with a handful of reporters.

Ko looked up at Chiu to say, "Call the old team."

Chapter 38

Toes

Fu's eyes were still sore when he unlocked his apartment door. He placed his bag on the chair next to the door and put away his coat. He turned on the TV in the small but clean-living room as he headed to the bathroom. The evening news was nothing but the shooting earlier that day. Fu stopped and watched. He undid his tie as the anchors talked over the details and their speculation. Fu moved to the bathroom as the younger reporter gave his best guess on the matter: revenge kidnapping. Fu opened the door to a fresh smell of peppermint from the new humidifier. He smiled at the smell and changed to his sleepwear as the younger anchor finished his speculation. Fu opened a drawer to fewer pill bottles than before to get his toothpaste as the senior anchor spoke the word triad.

Fu stepped out of the bathroom and gave the anchor his full attention, with toothpaste and toothbrush in hand.

"I believe this is an act of violence by the triad. Be it the victim owed them money or a 49er that needed to be disciplined, this to me screams triad."

His partner protested. "If that is so, then the police would have told us, but they said nothing on the matter. The anti-organized crime unit wasn't even there."

"But Inspector Ko was, and you may not remember, but Inspector Ko was in the anti-organized crime unit. He lived it and breathed it. No one else knows more about the triad than him, and he was there. Also, with Chief Executive Su at the helm, he doesn't want any talk of the triad as that would risk taking away funds from his new education reform."

"But Ko took care of that. Thousands of triad members were arrested after the massive operation he spearheaded with other police forces across Asia. There is no more triad."

Fu spat out his toothpaste quickly, to not miss the response.

"Oh, my boy, there will always be a triad. Yes, Executive Su's education reform could have the possibility of significantly reducing the number of new recruits to the triad with the rise in education in low poverty areas, which I will always be for. But it is taking too long. And yes, Inspector Ko and the rest of the law enforcement did a great job, but none of them arrested the real men behind it, the ones pulling strings and calling shots. Those are the people you need to bring in while you reform education. If we don't, this ancient evil will continue to live and continue to drag our sons and daughters int…"

Fu turned off the TV and looked around his small apartment. It seemed smaller with the new things he had bought: couch, TV, coffee table. He felt uneasy. He finished getting ready for bed and joined his sleeping wife. A new ultrasound picture sat on his nightstand. He could now see his daughter's toes. He slowly got into bed, so as to not wake his wife. She was finally sleeping better. He wrapped his arms gently around her as he reminded himself why he was doing this, to justify himself in front of his own conscience.

Chapter 39

White Truths

"So, I take it you've heard?" Lei Lei asked Jack as he got dressed for his date.

"Yeah, I thought you would be with Lóng, keeping him from going into a nervous breakdown."

Lei Lei chuckled as she walked into Jack's kitchen. "Too late for that." She placed her key to the apartment in her clutch purse that matched her floral sundrcss. "He's already making accusations toward the Suns, Mountains, Boqin. You name them, he thinks they did it."

Jack came out of the bathroom in a short-sleeved button shirt and khakis. He sat in a chair and slid his feet into brown dress shoes.

"The better question, though, is why are you all dressed up so nice?" Lei Lei leaned against the wall like she was modeling.

"I'm going on a date with Amy."

"What? When did this happen?" Her voice was giddy with excitement.

"A few days ago, before all this madness happened." Jack told the story as he tied his shoes and gathered up his things.

Lei Lei's eyes were fixed on Jack the entire time, listening intently. "Well, good for you. Damn, you two are going to be the perfect couple!" She squealed and grabbed his face and kissed him on the lips. "Now, once you get her in bed I want to know how she compares to me, alright?"

Jack laughed awkwardly. "Alright. I won't promise I can get back to you on that tonight, but I'll try soon." Jack headed to the door, his head bowed to hide his confusion.

"It shouldn't take long. Foreigners are always sexy." Lei Lei followed him out the door.

He chuckled as he locked his apartment up and changed subjects. "Is that the only reason you came by? To catch up on my love life?"

"It's not all about you. I also came by to get your thoughts on the kidnapping."

They walked toward the elevator.

"Why do you want a 49er's perspective?"

She stopped walking and faced Jack. "Please. That may be your title, but your knowledge and experience place you much higher. Those are just some of the reasons Lóng has been using you for more than just 49er errands. Also…" She started walking again. "Also, you're smart and could see something everyone else doesn't. So, thoughts?"

Jack called for the elevator and gave his answer with no hesitation. "The assassin."

The elevator dinged, and the doors opened.

"Interesting," Lei Lei's sexy face was gone again as her face went expressionless. "How do you think he knew to follow them?"

They entered the elevator and rode it to the ground floor.

"Probably the same way he was able to find Lóng the first time, I don't know."

Lei Lei glared off into space.

Jack continued, "With the things I saw him do, I wouldn't say it is out of his realm of possibilities."

Lei Lei's face didn't make any changes. She stayed silent as the rusty elevator made the only sound. Neither said anything else until they said their goodbyes when they both left the building. As he hailed a cab, Jack wondered if he was playing with fire, telling half-truths to make the lies seem more real. He wondered if this would get Guòqù in more danger. Mallory and fire flashed in front of his eyes again. He got in the cab and breathed slowly. He felt jealous of those undercover cops, as they had people to work with. All he had was himself and an iron-jawed assassin.

Chapter 40

Closed Doors

Fu still couldn't believe he had his own desk. His days of locker room smells and front desk duties were over, and he couldn't be happier. The desk was a little bare - only a computer, a picture of him and his wife, and the latest ultrasound of his daughter's toes - but it was a start. He wondered into a daydream about what his desk would look like in the coming months. That was pushed out of him when a fat man with slicked-back hair knocked on his desk.

"So, you're the lucky guy in the news?" he asked. His sleeves were rolled up over his thick arms. He leaned on Fu's desk. He wore no tie, but his badge on his belt ranked him a lot higher in the food chain than Fu.

"I wouldn't say lucky. Didn't really want to shoot him, but I had no choice."

The fat man chuckled under his breath, though his whole body moved like he was going to vomit. "I'd suggest you get to a white-collar crime division then or a higher end neighborhood because this precinct shoots a lot of bullets. Not since the mole, though." He looked off towards Ko's office just as Ko stepped out of it. "That may change, so, you may want to request that transfer soon."

The fat man stood up and walked toward Ko, who wasn't the only one leaving his office. Chiu was with him, as always, and Officer Cho. Ko greeted the fat man with a hug and led them all to the small conference room, where they closed the blinds. Fu wondered what the officer meant, and thoughts about telling Jack crossed his mind until his phone rang. It was his wife's new doctor. He smiled as he answered it, like it was an old friend. His attention shifted to the doctor and away from the shuttered conference room.

Inside the conference room, the group of men sat around a table and discussed how to take care of the triads once again.

"You know that Fu guy doesn't seem as bad as the way you make him out to be," said Niu, situating his massive body in a tiny chair.

"He's a brown-noser," responded Ko. He opened up his leather briefcase and slid yellow folders to everyone at the table.

"You're acting like an ass again. You've got to loosen up a little," said Niu.

"I'll loosen up when the triad is dealt with."

Niu started laughing. "Guess you'll just die an ass."

"Come on, man. Ko, you are sort of hard to him," commented Cho. He put on reading glasses for the folder, though he was the youngest in the meeting.

"I really don't care if I die an ass, as long as I take them down with me," said Ko.

Niu smiled as he thought of an inappropriate joke.

"Can we focus please?" Ko tried to get the meeting started. "Cho, I'm glad you can join us and take your father's place. He would be proud."

"Thank you. I'm glad to carry on the family work," Cho said as he opened the folder Ko gave him. "So, triads?"

"Yes," answered Ko. "I believe that we have more triads now than before our operation. I don't know how many yet, but I am assuming at least two new local ones, if not more. Our friends in China and Japan haven't had any trouble."

"So, because they haven't we will assume it isn't their triads traveling down here?" said Cho.

"Yes, because it would make more sense for them to recover on their own ground than somewhere else."

"Why three?" said Niu.

"Because of the recent activities," answered Ko. "The bus runner didn't work for the Red Dragon, and they have been attacked several times already."

"Why do you think they spawned?" asked Cho.

"Our clean-out left them questioning the Red Dragon's authority and left them to create their own new triad, thereby filling the void the Red Dragon left. That is why I think there are actually more than two, but that's just on a hunch."

Cho and Niu looked over the file a little longer. Chiu leaned back in his chair, his file still unopened as he knew the contents of it backward and forward. Niu was the first to close his, and asked, "Who is the American?"

"We don't know," answered Ko. "He was at the Little Bowl when we got calls of gunshots. He blocked us from getting upstairs. We haven't seen him since. Not sure how big of a role he plays, but if the Red Dragon is hiring aid outside Hong Kong, that means they could be getting desperate."

They nodded in agreement.

"That was my only question," said Niu. "So, I'm in. I think the evidence is still a little light, but if this thing is real, it could truly hurt this city. Again."

"You would be in if it meant another scratch on your pistol," commented Ko.

Niu laughed.

"Basically," Cho said, not looking up from his folder, "you are suggesting to bring the anti-organized crime section back up to full capacity, if not more. Correct?" Cho looked at Ko.

"Yes." Ko was straight with his answer.

"Okay. Have you talked to Su yet about this? Because you are talking about a lot of money." Cho's voice was concerned.

"Not yet, Chiu and I will be visiting him next week to get approval for it."

"And what if he doesn't give you it? Which is a possibility," Cho asked kindly.

"I hate to agree with the wet blanket, but he's right," added Niu. "Su has been sort of leading the finance reform to help fund his school project and has been cutting into all of our pockets a lot. What's this?" As Niu talked, Ko had brought out more files.

"This is what we do if Su doesn't agree with the plan." They all opened up the much thicker file. "A Plan B I hope we don't have to use."

Chapter 41

First Date

"Right here, wait a moment please," Jack told the cab driver as they approached Amy's building. She stood at the corner with her phone in her hand. Her attire was casual/dressy: tall black boots over skinny black jeans and a forest green shirt, loosely fit. Jack opened the car door and called to her. Once she saw him, she put her phone away and got in the cab, said hi to Jack, and quickly told the driver an address before returning her attention to Jack.

"So, how are you? Are you adjusting to your new place well?"

"As good as I can with only a few lamps and a mattress."

Amy giggled. The cab made great time through the afternoon traffic while Jack and Amy talked about his place. She was sketching out a rough floor plan of his loft as he explained it on her tablet. She dragged furniture icons from a different window on her tablet as she asked what kind of feel he wanted it to have. He named off many different attributes and feelings, but she was the one to mention 'homey'.

The cab stopped in front of a skyscraper with a gold outline to it. Jack followed Amy through the elegant hotel and up an elevator to the restaurant. The entire time she explained the design of the hotel and how she wished to be able to design a place like it. Immediately as they walked out of the elevator, the host waited on them, even taking their drink order as he led them to their table. They were seated near a window overlooking the entrance of the hotel. A waitress came by with their drinks and their first course. Jack relaxed back in his chair, and Amy brought out her tablet and started to show him her early ideas before he stopped her.

"Can we save those ideas until we get to the loft? It's going to make more sense to me when we are there."

"Sure." Amy closed her tablet up, observing Jack as he examined the museum-like paintings. "Long week?"

Jack gave a small smile. "You could say that. Business has been super busy and stressful. But I was all ready for discussing my loft until I sat down and…" Jack closed his eyes. "It just feels nice to relax."

"I know that feeling, too." She started reminiscing for half of the meal about the busiest week of her life. Jack didn't mind; he enjoyed any discussion that didn't include the triad, The Twelve, or his past.

They spent less than ten minutes actually talking about his loft. Amy did most of the talking as Jack did most of the listening. He interjected questions and comments that would make her laugh. Jack felt normal listening to her normal stories, her normal problems, her normal life. He felt jealousy seep into him. Thomas knew the role of Jack wasn't normal. But he wondered, even if he stopped The Twelve, if returning to Thomas could ever be normal. The wonder sailed away as his phone buzzed with a text from Yong. It gave an address and one word: "Tonight."

Chapter 42

Mahogany

A map of Hong Kong during the 1800's hung on the wall behind a large mahogany desk. Ko observed it carefully as he and Chiu waited in an office much nicer and bigger than theirs. The office included a seating area and a coffee table between couches and chairs. The room seemed to absorb the English-made map. The chairs, sofa, and coffee table were all made from English Oak trees with small floral patterns covering the seats. Chiu slowly spun the old globe around that sat in between two massive wall-sized windows overlooking the planted trees in front of the Central Government Complex.

The wooden double doors opened. A man taller than both inspectors stepped in. His face was clean shaven. His suit was more expensive than Ko's entire wardrobe. The man's lapel sported a gold pin of Hong Kong's flag.

"Ko, Chiu, so nice to see you both," said Su, the Chief Executive of Hong Kong. He closed the doors behind him and motioned to the couch. Ko and Chiu gave a low bow. "Please, have a seat, would you all like some tea?" Su walked over to his desk on the opposite side of the entrance.

"Yes, please. Thank you, sir," responded Ko sitting with Chiu on the couch. Su buzzed one of his secretaries to bring them tea, then sat across from them to chit-chat about the weather and sports. Soon the tea appeared, and they started to drink. The teapot was almost empty when Su asked them about their family.

"We halted the search for my brother's body yesterday," answered Ko.

Su lowered his eyes. "I'm sorry again for your loss. When will the funeral be?"

"I don't know yet, his wife… widow is planning it all out today."

"When you find out, will you let one of my secretaries know, because I want to pay my respects. Your brother's work in the force was a monumental blow to the triads across the world."

"It was," Ko responded softly. "But they're still out there."

Su shrugged as he leaned back. "Crime will always be out there."

"Yes, but the triads are still out there."

"Barely. The streets are cleaner from the drug-infested dealers it has had. They only occupy the poor districts on the east coast of the city. That is why we at the Executive Council came up with our multi-pronged attack focusing more officers in those areas while we get kids back in school." Su said this like he was reading off a teleprompter.

Ko nodded in agreement. "Yes, your education and infrastructure helped lower the poverty level, which made their market smaller."

"And the police have made the participants smaller as well. More than a thousand arrests in Hong Kong alone."

"That was years ago."

Su held his hand up. Ko stopped. Chiu kept silent, watching the back and forth. "What's your point, Ko? Do you think the triad killed your brother? I told him to move abroad, but he wouldn't listen. We all knew the risk of doing this, especially your brother."

Ko took a deep breath as he tightened and loosened his grip on his tea cup. "I know. But it's not that. It's the restaurant attack, back alley slashing, the bank robbery, the street shooting." Su's face was unchanged as Ko continued. "We haven't had a public shooting in years, and I think this is all because the Red Dragon is losing their grip. New, younger triads are stepping up to challenge their control."

"So?"

"BECAUSE THAT'S A TRIAD WAR!" yelled Ko, breaking the teacup in his hand. Pieces of it fell to the imported rug, followed by blood. Su was un-phased.

Chiu gave Ko a napkin, and continued where Ko left off. "We believe that if their activities go unchecked by the proper police force, these activities will increase as well as the body count of criminals, officers, and civilians. That is why we would like to request the increase of our anti-triad division funds back to one-hundred percent from the current position of twenty percent."

"If you wanted that, you should have gone through the Security Bureau like everyone else."

"Too much time," Chiu shot back.

"Well, I'm sorry, but I can't do that," Su responded without hesitation. "All the police funds are tied up pretty tight in their respective sectors and any extra money is going into the new schools." The two cops stared at him as he took the last sip of his tea and set the cup down on the coffee table. "Even if I could, you would still need to go through the proper channels with more than just hunches. I can't do personal favors anymore."

He stood up. Ko and Chiu followed suit, their eyes down. "I know it's hard," said Su, "what happened to your brother, but the triads aren't a major threat anymore. I think you give them too much credit, and that's probably because of how close to the line you were. Mind, I don't blame you. I would be looking over my shoulder too, after all you have been through."

Ko finished crafting the napkin into a bandage around his hand, and then said, "I would stop too if someone else paid the dues and I reaped the rewards." Ko turned and walked out of the office, ignoring the Chief Executive's hand.

After they had stormed out, Su stood and gazed out his windows while his secretary stepped in.

"I need someone to clean up the mess, replace the rug, and the teacup."

"Yes sir, anything else?"

"Have the interns draft a bill to extend the current finance plan for the police force to five years. I want it on my desk the day after tomorrow. It will be good practice for them."

The secretary bowed and left Su to himself and to Hong Kong.

Chapter 43

New Reason

Yong and the kid stood behind Heng as they rode up the elevator.

"I'm glad Lóng got the message. The weak ass bitch," said Heng. The elevator stopped and the doors opened to the same floor Yu died on. "We will meet in the same room as before." He snapped his fingers. "Gun? Where's Tin and Tan?" Heng looking around.

Yong handed him his gun and answered the question. "They're in the corner office with Lóng and his bodyguards."

Heng turned to face Yong. The kid flinched. "The bitch!" yelled Heng. "Why did he think he could decide the location?"

"I guess since you picked the building, he would pick the room."

Heng turned around and stomped toward the corner office. Following a few steps behind Heng, Yong leaned over and whispered to the kid, "Whatever happens, don't freak out. Okay?" The kid nodded, his eyes older now. They followed Heng a few steps behind as he walked through the new hallways with fresh drywall. Around a corner, Tin and Tan stood at the entrance of the office, their heads down as Heng stomped past them and through the black wood door. He gave no acknowledgment of them. The corner room was completely empty, which amplified the sunset scenery from the wall-sized windows. Heng strode into the middle of the large room and glanced around.

"Where is he?" he asked loudly.

The reply was the door shutting behind him. That was when he saw the other man, taller, fitter, and hairier than Heng. The man stroked his short, thick beard as he spoke. "Do you know who I am?"

Heng repositioned his feet to face the man head-on. "The Lumberjack I assume?" Heng looked him over. "No wonder they call you that."

The Lumberjack smiled. "That's one reason," Jack said. He pulled out a fire axe from behind his back. "Though today, you'll give it a new reason."

Heng pulled out his small gun and aimed it at the Lumberjack's forehead. "You should have worn a red flannel. That would have really helped the headlines." Heng pulled the trigger, and the gun clicked empty.

The Lumberjack looked out the window as if thinking of a response. He looked back and said, "Nah, too cliché." The Lumberjack walked closer, and Heng lowered his gun. Jack said, "What were you thinking? I mean, you should've known the Red Dragon wasn't going to just sit by and let you get away with this."

Heng stumbled backward. "What kind of leader lets his own brother get sliced up like that? Answer me that? I'll tell you: a weak one."

"Maybe," answered the Lumberjack.

Heng's back hit the window. Jack let his eyes wander to the parade outside in the distance. He was only able to see the parade dragon above anything else. He refocused on Heng. "Here's the thing: even with his faults, he's still got a lot more resources than you." The Lumberjack swung the axe up slowly and let gravity help it fall to his other hand.

"More resources than Boqin?" Heng said, panicked.

Jack stopped a few steps from Heng. "Yes."

"You sure? Let me live, and I'll tell you all I know."

"Or…" The Lumberjack released the axe with one hand and swung it down, implanting the blade into Heng's knee sideways. Heng cried in pain as his knee gave way under his weight. The axe head hit the ground, causing it to go even further into Heng's knee. "I just chop you up bit by bit before I kill you to show who has the real power in Hong Kong," the Lumberjack said, kneeling over Heng's body before pulling the axe out of Heng's knee.

Heng screamed through his teeth as he held his hands over the gash in his knee. "Maybe a little too late for that," Heng said, his face buried into the plywood floor.

"Why? Just because Boqin has a few Red Dragon traitors means he can challenge us?" The Lumberjack pushed Heng over with his axe to see his face.

"Because he has Tao," said Heng.

The Lumberjack grabbed Heng by the hair and pulled him close to his face. "Talk before I bleed you like a pig."

"Boqin called me, wanted me to join him, said Tao already joined so I should too."

The Lumberjack let go of Heng's hair and stood up. Heng's head hitting the floor echoed through the empty room. He stared at Heng for a few moments as tears rolled down Heng's face and the blood spread to the Lumberjack's shoes.

"That's it?" the Lumberjack finally asked. "He privately told you Tao joined him? Have you ever heard of this little thing called lying?"

"It wasn't private," said Heng. "Tao was in the call too."

Chapter 44

The Box

Jack's hand popped out of the room Heng entered moments ago and ordered for the shoe box. When the kid gave Jack the cardboard shoe box, he noticed blood on Jack's sleeve. Jack closed the door again, and they all stood in silence. The kid observed Yong, who was drumming his fingers as they waited, and asked, "Are you in charge now?"

Yong stopped drumming his fingers. Tin and Tan looked up at Yong to see his response. "No, the Dragon Head is."

The door opened, and Jack stepped out with the box in his hands. His suit was spotted with blood. His gloves were soaked. "Wrap the body up and dispose of it," he said. Jack placed the closed box on the ground and stepped aside to let Tin, Tan, and the kid in. The kid vomited when he caught a glimpse of his former boss's body.

"Get going," Jack demanded, "you can vomit when you get home," Jack closed the door behind the kid. Jack took off his latex gloves and placed them in the outside pockets of his suit, before stripping that off too.

"Did you know about Tao?" Jack asked, handing Yong his suit jacket.

Yong placed the coat in a trash bag. "What about him?"

"He's with Boqin." Jack took off his pants and dumped them in the trash bag.

"Shit," said Yong.

"Boqin was trying to leverage that to get Heng to join him."

"I didn't know anything about that."

"I'm not surprised, it happened yesterday." Jack took off his white undershirt and gym shorts that he wore under his suit. "Guess Boqin heard about our failure and wanted to take advantage of it." Jack looked down at the box, while Yong stuffed the rest of Jack's clothes into the trash bag. "Give me your burn phone, I'll get you a new one," ordered Jack. Yong handed Jack an old silver flip phone.

Jack dialed and hardly waited for a second before speaking. "Hey, can he talk?"

Yong placed the bag by the box against the wall and watched Jack curiously. Jack said into the phone, "Hey, do you need that package or can I send it to a friend?"

Yong tried to eavesdrop on what the response was but couldn't as Jack turned and walked away from him in nothing but boxers.

Jack continued his side of the phone conversation. "He recently got a new roommate, and I wanted to congratulate him… A big fellow… Yeah, he suffered… Thanks." Jack hung up and tossed the phone to Yong. "You will get a new one in a few weeks, burn it and the clothes."

Yong handed Jack a duffle bag with gym clothes that Jack quickly threw on.

"Aren't you afraid this will start a war?" asked Yong.

Jack finished putting on his clothes and grabbed the box, saying as he left, "This isn't for Boqin."

Chapter 45

New Beginnings

"I love your new place, very modern," said Tao as he sat in Boqin's new house. The living room's windows overlooked Deep Water Bay toward the forest-covered Middle Island.

"I'm not fond of the windows, though," said Zemin. "Too much exposure." He was sitting opposite of Tao on a black couch.

"You worry too much," said Enlai, seated to Zemin's right.

"No, just an observation, always check your blindsides," said Zemin.

Enlai chuckled at his younger brother and said, "He's right."

Boqin came around the corner carrying an old silver tray with a new white tea set and said, "That's why I had all the glass in the house replaced with bulletproof glass."

Zemin relaxed a little more in his seat. Boqin placed the tray on the glass coffee table and started to pour tea for his guests. As he handed them each a cup on a saucer, he said, "I take it you all are also settling into your new homes as well?"

"I am at least. When did you go into the real estate business?" Enlai asked.

"A few years ago," Boquin said. "Diversifying your interest is always safer than putting everything into one business. Besides being a great money maker, it comes with super cheap homes for you and your brothers." After serving everyone, Boqin sat down with his tea at the opposite end of the coffee table from Enlai. "Speaking of, how are you all?"

Enlai started. "Great so far. I wasn't fond of losing one of the bus routes, but the taxi cabs have picked up the extra slack and then some. Also, I've been very successful using them as drug runners. A few days ago, I was able to move more than twenty-thousand dollars' worth of cocaine and heroin around to my dealers."

"Good," said Boqin, though he didn't seem that impressed. "How are your dealers handling that much inventory?"

"Alright. I'm going to have to start slowing it down if they don't start moving it faster."

"I don't think you will need to slow that down." Boqin took a yellow dry erase marker out of his blue polo's breast pocket. "What about you, Zemin?"

"I'm alright," said Zemin. "My protection rackets are doing alright, and I've also started to expand to some lower level apartment complex with the extra money from the bank hit."

"Good, good, Tao?" Boqin took out a blue marker.

"Went out on a scout for some new girls since I haven't had some young blood in a while but came up pretty short since I don't have that many suppliers since the mole."

Boqin took out the last two markers, green and red, and said, "That was a bad year, but also a good year in the long run." A door opened behind them, and footsteps echoed through the empty halls. "As it freed us all from our old authority."

Gui walked into the room, his thin arms lifted up like he was about to hug the entire room. "Brothers! How are we?"

Shock and confusion covered all the faces except for Boqin's, who stood up and embraced him.

"I thought you were in prison?" asked Enlai, standing with the others to greet him.

"I was," said Gui, "but thanks to the help of some new friends I got out early and got reconnected with Boqin as I laid low outside of Hong Kong." Gui sat down in Boqin's chair. "This feels like a reunion of Red Dragon misfits."

"What kind of friends?" asked Zemin.

"Powerful friends," stated Boqin as he started writing their names in a line on the window with his markers. "And with that, we have our triad." His name was the only one absent from the window. "And this is where we start."

Boqin pulled out a black dry erase marker from his pocket and began to write occupations under the names. Gui got a supplier. Enlai was the runner, Tao, the dealer, and Zemin, the protector. Boqin connected the names with arrows like a typical business supply chain. He then drew a circle around it, with Zemin's name just outside of the chain. He took a step back so his Red Poles could see it in its entirety. They all nodded as it fell into place.

"Now, there is some room for mixing it up," said Boqin, "as I know Zemin will want to deal with his own apartments by his people. And as we expand you all will need to be ready to promote your own 49ers to take Red Pole positions around the city as we will be focusing on the bigger picture. But, that is it." Boqin stepped back with pride to admire his work.

"This really changes it up," commented Tao.

"Does it, though?" Boqin responded. "When we were under the Red Dragon's foot, this is what they used, but we were just too little to see it. We've all been doing well so far, but this,"

Boqin tapped on the window, "this can make us soar. All we need to do is focus on what we are best at."

"It wasn't this, West-ish," said Tao.

Enlai voiced his concern before Boqin replied to Tao. "What is Gui supplying?"

Gui's thin face stretched as he smiled. "Everything. Do you want girls? Boys? Weed? Cocaine? Heroin? Acid? I can literally get anything."

"Sounds too good to be true," said Zemin. "Where is all of it coming from?"

Boqin stepped in. "That's confidential. All I can say is, it's a third party that is global."

His Red Poles were reserved in their faces as they looked at the window and Boqin's plan.

"Look," Gui quickly breaking the silence before it grew into more uncertainty, "I already got some of everything to give you all a taste. No wasted time in looking, no wasted resources or energy on opium gum. Just the finished product. Young slaves, new weapons, excellent drugs. I'll have your personal choice delivered to your home soon."

Lust in their eyes grew as they dreamt.

"I know you all have suppliers," said Boqin, picking up where Gui had left off. "This supplier will far surpass any other supplier. They can offer more with a greater diversity and a lower price than any of your guys. Because if we are going to sweep away the smaller groups of idiots, dealers, pimps, and the Red Dragon, then we need to outpace them with our drugs, our whore houses, and our weapons. Once we have them bleeding by a thousand cuts, we will stretch our claws outwards as the most powerful triad in Hong Kong. The White Tiger."

Gui's face grimaced as he said, "Are we actually calling ourselves that?"

Chapter 46

A Package

Tao thought long and hard as he was driven back home. The afternoon talks with The White Tiger rolled around his mind as he stared out at the high-end suburb where he lived. The porch lights shone out in the dark night. He thought about this new process, this new hierarchy, and wondered if he was doing the right thing.

Or the most profitable thing.

His mind roamed to the new suppliers. Boqin and Gui played it very close to the chest, and he didn't like that. The car pulled into his gated driveway. The driveway was lined with cherry trees on both sides, and even at night, he could still make out the pink blossoms. The car drove up to the front door, where several guards stood. Two had dogs, while the rest stood at attention. He tried to see the problem, but saw nothing out of the ordinary until the car was right in front of his house. That is when he saw the opened shoe box on his doorstep.

He said no words as he exited the car. His eyes did not wander from the box as he approached it. The closer he grew to it, a faint odor rose, an odor of decay. His guards didn't move as he stopped and looked into the box. The only sound in the entire courtyard was the dogs panting behind him. Tao clenched his fists.

"When did it arrive?" he demanded under his breath, his eyes not breaking with the box.

"This afternoon," said the guard to Tao's right.

"Who delivered it?"

"No one knows. A blue lantern took it and placed it on the doorstep without thinking. Once the dogs checked it out, we opened it and haven't touched it since."

"Bring him to me," Tao said calmly as he kneeled down and gazed at the face of Heng's decapitated head. Footsteps on concrete rang out with no echo behind them. A baby-faced teenage boy standing with his face down met Tao.

"What were you thinking, bringing an unordered, unknown package to my doorstep?" Tao's questions were calm but authoritative.

"I, I, didn't know about our system, my, my…"

Tao cut him off. "What if it was a bomb?"

"I, I, didn't think of that since that's a dirty western way-"

"Your arrogance will not save you." Tao walked down the few steps toward him. "Our world is rapidly changing." Tao stood right in front of him, glaring at his bowed head and softly shaking body. "And we need men who can adapt, not boys who can't." Tao snapped his fingers and walked away as all the guards drew their knives and killed the boy by a thousand cuts, more or less. The dogs stayed seated and waited for the guards to be done with their dinner.

Once inside, Tao called Boqin immediately and informed him of the situation. Boqin didn't interrupt him once. Tao paced back and forth in his upstairs study until he was finished talking and then sat in his desk chair, rubbing the leather armrest and staring at a screen saver of a small ball bouncing around and changing colors.

Boqin finally spoke. "Well, we can manage without him."

Tao sat up. "And?"

"And we aren't going to respond yet,"

"What the-" Tao began to curse but Boqin stopped him and reminded him of his place.

"Do not curse in my presence," demanded Boqin. "I am your superior, I am the head of this triad and I say we don't do anything. Start thinking like a Red Pole or I will replace you with someone who will." Boqin hung up.

Tao threw his cell phone across the room, making a mark in the door. Tao cursed at the empty room for a full minute. He caught his breath as his mind moved a thousand different thoughts around as his anger still burned for his new boss - though Tao could tell Boqin had a boss above him.

"It's the Red Dragon all over again," Tao said to himself. His thoughts grew slower as they converged to their final destination. Caring not of the consequences or the cost, but to take matters into his own hands and avenge his friend.

Chapter 47

Fishing

Guòqù's memories trickled back into him as he gazed into the open sea. Then one particularly intact memory rushed upon him, and he was there again, on a lonely island so long ago. Sand moving between his toes. An old freight ship toppled over on the beach. Dead employees of The Twelve laid scattered on the beach as the birds picked him. And, possibly disconcertingly, Guòqù's clean and intact face smiling at the sight.

The old motorboat sparked and brought him back to the present. Guòqù stopped the boat on the strangely calm bay. Guòqù's prisoner was unconscious on the floor of the vessel, with his shoulder wound neatly bandaged. Guòqù's leg was wrapped as well. A sewn-up patch covered the bullet hole on his torn pants. He watched as a small school of fish came to investigate his boat. He watched them carefully, like a cat about to swipe. Memories of the island came back to his mind.

The prisoner made a sound.

The school of fish quickly scattered. Guòqù turned his attention to the 49er as he awoke. The prisoner tried to sit up but couldn't due to his bound hands and feet. He started shaking violently for a few moments, before seeing Guòqù at the head of the boat. Guòqù's face covered, the prisoner's eyes moved frantically, trying to make sense of the shadowy figure sitting on the edge of the ship. Guòqù let the prisoner look long enough for the silence to set in and his curiosity to take more hold than fear.

"What do you want?"

"Where's Lóng?" Guòqù asked calmly.

"Who?" The prisoner's lie was thin and weak.

Guòqù lifted his Jō off his shoulder and drove it into the floor of the boat. Water quickly flowed in.

"What the shit?" The prisoner tried to move but couldn't as he was zip tied to the boat.

Guòqù asked again, no change in his voice as his combat boots got wet.

"I don't know man! They didn't tell me!"

Guòqù asked again, the water covering his feet now.

"I don't know! I was just a guard!" shouted the 49er as the salt water came to his shoulder. Guòqù impaled the boat again. The front of it was descending faster but Guòqù was still unmoved as the sea came up his shins and engulfed the 49er's ears.

"Where is Lóng?" asked Guòqù, unfazed by the water.

The 49er strained to keep his face out of the sea. "I don't know!"

Guòqù didn't ask again and just watched as the sea slowly engulfed the 49er's head and the front of the boat. The shouting and cussing quickly turned to drowned out yells, with bubbles replacing the curses. By the time he stopped screaming, three-fourths of the vessel was submerged, with Guòqù calmly floating in the sea. He waited only a few moments till he dived under and pulled the thug free, breaking the wood and some bones. Once the prisoner's head was above water he coughed loudly in Guòqù's face, salt water spraying him.

Guòqù asked him again for the final time. "Where is Lóng?"

Snot dripped down the 49er's face as he caught his breath. "The pier. We were going to the east pier to drop off the package on a boat named Koporso, that's all I…"

Before he could even beg, Guòqù pushed his head back under until the prisoner stopped struggling, and his dead body floated up. Guòqù swam back to shore to start seeking out the ship named Koporso. He had a small smile under his steel jaw, just like that day on the beach.

Chapter 48

Recap

Once Jack was done telling Lei Lei what happened, she said nothing for a full minute. She didn't break eye contact or blink as she stood in the unfinished bar area of Jack's apartment. Two guards stood at the door, while Jack leaned on the bar island next to her. He tried to break the silence, but just as his lips moved, Lei Lei punched him.

"Are you trying to start a war?" she asked. Jack didn't answer, but lowered his head and posture and waited for her to finish, and so she continued. "I don't give two shits what they have done to us or if Lóng gave you the ok! The blows they are throwing have no threat behind them! Boqin is just trying to be a show-off, get us scared. We needed to take those small hits so we can get ready to hit him back."

Jack was unable to stay silent. "Yu was a small hit? Have you talked to your brothers?"

"Yes! We don't have the resources to go against them in a fully-fledged war! I'm the only one here who isn't getting blinded by emotions. That's why I am helping Lóng and Li." Lei

Lei sounded as though she thought she was getting through to him.

"If it came down to it, we can get what we need," said Jack. She sighed at his calm response, and so he continued. "We have the numbers and are still more organized than they are at the moment. If we'd done nothing, we would have been seen as even weaker, and the small hits would've grown to bigger ones."

"Jack, you don't know about Tao and Heng's relationship, do you?" Lei Lei asked calmly. Jack shook his head, unsure where she was going. She explained, "I can do a lot of things, pull a lot of strings, but I'm near the end of strings I can pull. Our funds are starting to go dry." Her voice was calm and together. "We need time to build our stash again, and I can't deal with an angry Tao right now."

Jack folded his arms and lowered his head.

"Don't worry," said Lei Lei, "we will get those bastards, and they will die by a thousand cuts - but till then, no more aggressive movements. No more recruiting. We just sit tight and do business while I take care of Tao." Lei Lei grabbed her purse and left with her bodyguards. Before the door even closed, she walked back in and added, "Last thing, don't forget to pick up the cash from our whore house. No one has gone to pick it up in a while since all this madness happened."

"No, problem. I'll do it tomorrow night."

Lei Lei lingered for a few moments before thanking him and leaving. Jack didn't wait long until Guòqù walked out of the restroom.

"Just out of curiosity," said Jack, "what would you have done if she needed to use the restroom?"

Guòqù ignored the question and skipped to his business. "I have a name. A boat called Koporso."

Jack nodded. "Makes sense. He would stay on the move, and it would be tough to sneak up on him."

"No, it won't," Guòqù said as he removed his damp mask. He grabbed a kitchen towel and started to wipe his face and steel mouthpiece dry.

"Anyway," said Jack, "Lei Lei - do you think she knows about them?"

Guòqù shook his head. Jack leaned against the kitchen counter, and Guòqù finished drying. "What if Lei Lei does know about them, and they are telling her to avoid the war?" said Jack.

"Possible. But war can be very profitable."

"Only if they are selling to both sides."

Guòqù sat down on a bar stool and scratched his cheek right above his steel jaw. "Not outside their realm. But they work better with fewer people knowing. They would have told Lóng not to tell a soul, even on his deathbed."

Jack leaned forward, his eyes focused on Guòqù's eyes. "Not even his heir?"

"No." Guòqù stood up as he realized the situation. Jack looked off into the distance thinking as Guòqù put on his sweater. "I'll find Lóng," said Guòqù as he headed toward the door.

"But what if he doesn't know?"

Guòqù didn't stop to answer and was gone as fast as he came in. Jack stood there alone, again. He thought how The Twelve would play this all out to their advantage: for their profit, of course, but of more than money. Jack knew it was for the power. The more he thought about it, the more it made sense. As an organization like this, it would be simple for them to put on different faces and names to sell the weapons and then step back and watch their plan play out. He shook his head and took off his shirt as he headed toward his bedroom. His thoughts went back to why have competition when you can have a monopoly of it all. As Jack got into bed, he felt like he was missing something, like the motives were too simple.

Money and power.

He closed his eyes and fell to sleep, mulling over it for some time as he followed what Crumwell told him to do: play the part. A hint of fear came over him as he hoped he wasn't playing the part of Jack too well. He wished his training had taught him how to find himself after the mission was over.

Chapter 49

Sea Serpent

Li sat on the deck of the Koporso drinking his favorite cheap beer and watching the sunset. Lóng's voice could be heard talking to Lei Lei over the phone. Li thought about Yu's death again. He felt better, but still grieved for him, one of his dearest friends. Two guards stood on the balcony above Li, talking about the newest superhero movie. One thought it was the greatest while the other thought it was just okay, which the first one took much more as a personal offense than just an opinion. Li paid no attention to either of them. He closed his eyes for just a minute. He faded into a soundless sleep just as the guards stopped talking about superheroes abruptly. Lóng said goodbye to Lei Lei a few seconds later, leaving the ship in a peaceful state and letting Li sleep peacefully, too.

The sound of something splashing the water awoke Li. He faintly heard the sound of soothing music playing behind him. The sun was far gone, and the light to the deck was off. The only light was through the glass windows behind him. He slowly stood up, a little groggy, and walked inside. He watched his feet and rubbed his eyes as he opened the door and entered a nightmare. Lóng's personal bodyguards laid across the table in the middle of the room. Their heads and the table were covered in blood. The bartender was on the floor, his feet poking out from behind the bar. Lóng was on the bar itself, his chest covered in blood. Li rushed over to his side, almost tripping over his own feet. Li shouted Lóng's name as he observed the wounds. A large cut had been made on his chest, stretching from his left shoulder to his right hip. Li didn't stare too long at it as he saw bones and organs moving in the cut. He ripped his shirt off and pressed it over the cut. Lóng coughed up blood, his whole-body jolting, his broken arms swinging.

"Liao! Holy shit, you're alive! Who was it?"

"Li… Li listen, listen," Lóng's voice was soft and groggy. Li stopped. "It was… Assassin…Wanted…Call them…" He coughed again.

"Who? Lei Lei?"

Lóng mouthed no. "Twelve… Flash drive." Lóng's voice quivered in fear.

"Twelve? Twelve flash drives?"

Lóng shook his head and with his last breath said, "Password." He tilted his head back and looked up. Li followed his eyes, down the bar to a thirteen-digit number carved into the wood. Li thought of his flash drive that he plucked from the dead hitman's hand in Spain. Li looked back at him to ask more questions, but Liao Shang Lóng was already dead.

Chapter 50

Blood

The whore house threw Jack into a déjà vu moment. The house was more modern and cleaner than the one in Amsterdam; the freshly painted green door seemed to pop out of the old building. The windows were painted black, with colored lights shining out of them and a few girls' silhouettes dancing in the window.

Fu got off the bus outside his apartment, a smile on his face as he remembered their anniversary on his own.

Tao and a group of his 49ers got into a black SUV.

Jack knocked on the door and waited. A guy on a bicycle, paying attention to only the windows, passed behind him. A man in his fifties opened the door to Jack. The man's colorful Hawaiian shirt was unbuttoned revealing his hairless chest. He let Jack in without any hesitation.

Fu, smelling the flowers he got for his wife and peeking at dinner in the paper bag, rode the elevator up to his floor.

Tao instructed his men on the plan as their driver paid extra attention to the traffic laws around him.

Jack followed the middle-aged man through the living room. They passed a teenage girl in her underwear dancing in front of the purple lamp pointed at the window. She seemed bored by it all. The second room was separated by paper-thin room separators. Each small section housed a tattered fabric chair. A couple of sections had girls entertaining customers with seductive dance moves and emotionless faces.

Fu's elevator arrived at his floor with a ding. He exited to a deserted floor as usual.

Tao and his 49ers parked a few blocks away from their destination.

Jack walked up a flight of stairs to the second floor. Pictures covered the staircase, pictures of their best girls showing more skin than anything else. The smell of cigarettes and sweat grew stronger with every step as he approached the second floor.

Fu walked up to his door and sat down his dinner to reach his keys.

Tao and his personal bodyguard turned the safety off on their used handguns as the rest sharpened their knives before exiting the SUV.

Jack walked past closed doors of several rooms that had no customers. Jack found this a little odd as they entered the corner room on the floor. This room was bare besides a plastic card table and a potbellied man sitting at it counting the day's earnings.

Fu opened the door and picked up the paper bag, saying with a cheery voice, "Happy Anniversary!"

Tao and his 49ers reached the entrance.

"I know, I know you are here for the payments," said the man as he pushed his metal chair back and stood up, "but how about this?" Jack rolled his eyes. The fat man continued while the man in the flowered shirt leaned against the door frame. "Hear me out," said the fat man. "You let me keep a little extra, and I'll let you sleep with a fresh one." He walked to another door to Jack's right and opened it.

"Fu?" responded Fu's wife. Her voice was not near as chipper as his.

Tao knocked on the door.

The fat man stood in the doorway and said, "This girl is super out of it, but those can be the best ones. A real human doll to play with." When Jack shook his head, the fat man added, "You can't say no to something you haven't seen." He smiled maliciously, obviously thinking himself clever for thinking that up.

Fu walked with a quick step to see his wife sitting on the floor leaning against the couch in a pool of her own blood and water.

The freshly painted green door opened to Tao.

Jack rolled his eyes and walked over to the open the door to look at the poor girl. He prepared himself to hold his frustration and disgust back. That wasn't what he needed to hold back.

Thomas saw her outside his mind for the first time in six months, clear and pristine, just like the night he proposed. He saw Mallory.

Epilogue

Two different numbers shined on the middle monitor on a wall of screens. One a phone number, and the other an IP address. An older man sat in a black leather chair in his bathrobe, watching the numbers. The door behind him slid open, and a young man in a new suit walked in and bowed. Keeping his head low, the young man waited for the man at the monitor to give a command. The man in the chair rolled a little glass ball in his hand with a map of South Asia reflecting out of it.

Finally, the older man voiced his question: "Is it him?"

"The voice is the best match we have had," said the young man. "We still don't have visual confirmation yet."

The older man huffed out a chuckle. "We were lucky to get a voice." He placed the glass ball on his armrest where it sat cozily on its own platform, and then he said, "Li must be the next number, poor thing."

"Did you receive the news about the whore house?" the boy timidly asked.

"Yes," replied the older man. "I was hoping it wouldn't happen this fast or violently. I want you to call in Red to fix that. And call in the asset to take care of his family matters. I'll inform the rest of The Twelve."

36303084R00109

Made in the USA
Columbia, SC
24 November 2018